Knife edge

My mind whirls, cogs turning. I don't want to go and watch some crappy football match. But if it's Derby, he's a real Derby fan, never used to miss a game. He might risk it, might come to the match, might not be able to resist. And if he's there, I'll spot Him. I'll find Him, talk to Him, make Him think I want to see Him. I'll have to be crafty, as crafty as Him. I'll arrange to meet Him somewhere quiet, and then. . .

My heart thumps with excitement. I feel blood rush to my cheeks. I look at Eric and give a quick nod.

He beams. "Oh, that's great."

Jill looks happier too. "So, no more running away, David?" she asks.

I'm only too happy to nod. And I don't mind being banished to my room when Jill says I need an early night. I can lie in bed and think up a new plan. This is my first piece of good luck. Perhaps I won't have to go and find Him – he just might come to me.

Other titles by Sylvia Hall:

No Fear

Point

KNIFE
edge

Sylvia Hall

■SCHOLASTIC

For Alex and James

Scholastic Children's Books,
Commonwealth House, 1–19 New Oxford Street,
London, WC1A 1NU, UK
A division of Scholastic Ltd
London ~ New York ~ Toronto ~ Sydney ~ Auckland
Mexico City ~ New Delhi ~ Hong Kong

First published in the UK by Scholastic Ltd, 2003

Copyright © Sylvia Hall, 2003

ISBN 0 439 97816 5

Printed and bound in Great Britain
by Cox & Wyman Ltd, Reading, Berkshire

1 2 3 4 5 6 7 8 9 10

The right of Sylvia Hall to be identified as the author of
this work has been asserted by her in accordance with the
Copyright, Designs and Patents Act, 1988.

one

If I keep my eyes closed they'll think I'm asleep. They can't make me talk.

David, David, have a sip of this.

I'm thirsty but I let the water dribble down my chin.

David, wake up, there's a good lad.

I lie still as a plank letting their words slur over me. Voices mutter, footsteps squeak.

David, look who's come to see you.

I don't need to open my eyes. I know who it is. I've heard her voice, sickly sweet, trickling down like syrup. *Are you comfortable? Is there anything I can get you?*

No. Go away.

It's been a shock for you. I'm here to help. If you'll just open your eyes and talk to me.

Her voice shivers to a stop. I slide my head sideways, flick open my eyelids and stare up at her. She flinches and blinks. I hope she feels guilty. I hope she's in big trouble. She was the one supposed to protect us; keep us safe.

I'm in the garden, near the gate. There's a noise. *Pop, pop, bang, pop* – sharp explosions in the street. A souped-up rust bucket squeals round the corner – red and silver, shiny as a Coke can, long-nosed bonnet, headlamps like satellites. My heart rams up against my ribs and I know. Even before it stops, even before the door creaks open, I know. I stand with fists clenched, nails razoring my palms and watch him step out.

"Hey, Davey. Long time no see. Blimey, you've grown. Want to come for a ride?"

His face eager, thinking I'll be excited. As if I cared about riding with him. I'd sooner have a black eye.

"Get stuffed. Shove off," I say.

He laughs, then turns and reaches into the back seat, pulls out a bunch of flowers.

I move to the gate, plant my feet behind it; defiant, glaring. "You can't come near us – the court said."

"Don't be silly. I only want to give her these." He thrusts out an arm, fingers grip the top of the gate, knuckles hard and bony. "Just want to say Happy Birthday."

Before he can push the gate open I turn and run up the path, fly into the house, slam the door.

"Mum, he's here," I yell. "It's Him."

Mum hurries from the kitchen, face slashed with

fear. I push the latch down and shove my back against the door. *Thump, thump* – deep shuddering thuds shake my shoulders.

Mum's hands fly to her throat. "God help us," she whispers. *Smash* – a kick splinters the wood.

"It's no use," she says. "I'll have to let him in."

"No, Mum. No."

With a trembling hand she plucks at her skin. "He'll break the door down if I don't."

I grab her wrist. "We could get the table, use it as a barricade."

She shakes her head, pulling away. "You know what he's like, he'll find a way in." Her hand brushes my hair as she feels for the latch. "Don't worry. I'll handle him."

My world stops. Everything stands still. No sound, nothing. Heaviness presses down on me, I can hardly breathe. I know what's coming. "Mum," I plead, but she's already undoing the catch.

The door swings inwards with him behind it, panting, eager as a dog ready for its dinner. I want to hit him. Find a stick. *Wham! Bang!* See his head split open.

"Must've been stuck," he says, nodding at the shuddering door.

I stare at him, my eyes burning, then I glare at Mum. If she hadn't opened the door, he might have gone away.

"Hello Alison. Happy Birthday." He pushes the

flowers in Mum's face. "You didn't think I'd let your birthday go by without seeing you, did you?" His voice is soft. "Took me ages to find you." He smiles. "It was worth it, though."

I crease up as Mum smiles back at him; it's only the plastic smile she wears for the social worker but he thinks it's real.

"I knew you'd be glad to see me, Ali," he says. "Ridiculous us being apart, should never have happened." She starts to back away from him but he grabs her shoulder. "Don't go. Let me look at you." He holds her at arm's length, examining her, his eyes sweeping up and down. "Sometimes I forget how beautiful you are. Those lovely star-blue eyes. Here, let me give you a birthday kiss."

My guts explode as he pulls her close. Bite his tongue Mum, bring your knee up, squash his balls. But she doesn't. She just stands there and lets him paw her and he's whispering and slurping, lapping it up.

So you're not going to talk to me, David? Well, I can understand that. I'm not sure I'd want to speak either. But when you're feeling better I want you to try and tell us what happened at the house. Can you remember, David?

Course I remember – how can I forget? It plays over and over, images flashing inside my head, like a video on rewind; backwards, forwards; I can't stop it – the pictures burning into my brain.

4

Mum moves into the kitchen. "The flowers are lovely. I'll put them in water. I was going to make a cup of tea. Would you like one?" Her voice is calm but brittle as biscuits.

He follows her. "You are pleased to see me, aren't you, Ali?"

Over his shoulder I see Mum's mouth fold into a tight line, her eyes half close and she stiffens as he touches her hair.

I step forward, fists clenched, ready to punch him. I don't know if he notices me but suddenly he drops his hand.

"Tell you what, I'm hungry, I've had nothing to eat all day," he says loudly as he smacks Mum on the bottom. "Make me one of your great fry-ups, Ali." He laughs, a deep throaty chuckle. "Then we'll send David off somewhere while you and me have a real birthday treat."

I know what he means, dirty sod. I scowl at him as he lights up a fag and sits down. He doesn't take his eyes off Mum as she opens cupboards, searching for something to put the flowers in. When she's found a big mug, she fills it with water, cuts the stalks with scissors and fidgets about with the stems.

"Nice, aren't they," he says. "I got the colours you like."

Mum nods.

He leans back, flicks ash on the floor. Mum carries on

twitching the flowers and he starts to look annoyed. "Come on, Ali, they'll do. Where's the food? I'm starving."

She gives him a wide berth as she sets the flowers in the middle of the table. They glow like a trophy, a flash of colour in the drab room. I hate them. I hate friggin' flowers.

He's lost interest in them too. He blows smoke over them. "So, tell me, what've you been up to?" he asks.

Mum doesn't answer, she puts her head down and makes herself busy, getting out the frying pan, opening the fridge. "Do you want one egg or two?"

"You know me Ali, I'm a two-egg man," he says with a wry smile.

Mum lights the gas, drops slices of bacon into the frying pan. They sizzle and the smell fills the room. Stop it, Mum, stop it.

I stamp into the connecting room and slump on to the sofa, covering my ears, trying to blot out everything that's happening in the kitchen, but it doesn't work. I can still hear him rattling on, asking Mum how she is, then he starts telling her how he's missed us and gone round the streets trying to find us, showing our photo to loads of people. What photo? The one where we're all smiling like a happy family and Mum's make-up is hiding the bruises? I hate him, I sodding hate the greasy git.

Between mouthfuls of tea he gives Mum some crap about how he's changed. "I'm a new man, Alison. I've reformed. No gambling, no boozing, don't touch a drop."

I think of all the times he dragged me off to the boozer, left me sitting outside; remember all the times he came home tanked up and belted Mum. I hope he chokes.

"Got a good job now, Ali. Been there six months, selling conservatories. Involves me in quite a bit of travelling. That car out there, that's just temporary – boss has me down for a new Escort."

I peer over the sofa and see him chomping away, cheeks bulging with food. When he's finished he wipes his mouth on his hand then he leans back and smoothes his hair. He's vain about his hair, always combing and quiffing it, thinks he's a ruddy walkin' shampoo advert. When he catches me looking at him, he stretches his arms, cracks his knuckles and stands up.

"Not a bad place this. Plenty of space. We could make a new start here, Ali – you and me."

He wanders about, touching things like he owns the place. He takes off his leather jacket, hangs it on the back of the chair, picks up my drawing pad and leafs through it.

"Hey, these are good," he says.

I rush forward and snatch the drawings off him. "Leave them alone. They're mine."

"You should show them to somebody. You've got talent, kid." He laughs. "Take after your Dad, eh?"

Oh yeah, we all know what talents you've got. Drinking yourself silly, falling over, making a prat of yourself. You make me sick. I hate it when people say I'm like you. I try every way to be different – crop my hair, stoop so I look shorter, squint to hide the colour of my eyes. I'm not like you one bit and you can't draw for toffee so leave my stuff alone.

While I'm thinking this I give him the dead eye and eventually he registers that I don't want to talk to him and he shrugs and walks away, turning his attention to Mum instead. She's busy splashing water in the sink and he goes and stands next to her.

"Have you missed me Ali, have you? Is there a chance for us? Can't be easy on your own." His hands slide over her body. "I've missed you," he says. He pulls her close, whispers in her ear then he starts to push her gently towards the stairs.

I see the frightened look on Mum's face and anger surges through me. I step forward trying to block his path. "Can we go for a ride in the car?" I ask.

"Not now, Davey."

"Why not?" I ask, stubbornly.

He glares furiously.

"Why not?" I ask again.

He sucks in a big breath of air, then blows it out as he elbows me out the way. Mum's face is white, her fingers flutter like frenzied butterflies, I can't bear to see her but I can't look away. I grip my drawing pad, my hands rigid with tension. "Leave her alone!" I yell.

His foot is on the bottom step but he snaps round, eyes flaring. My stomach clenches, turns inside out. I've done it now. I swallow hard, waiting. I wish I could rush him – he's not that big, not bloody Superman. I could take him by surprise, punch him, wind him before he knew what was coming. But I daren't move, none of us moves; the air around us crackles with tension, we stand in a silence cold as the moon. I'm aware of his mad gold eyes, luminous as a cat's, I'm almost hypnotized by them, they glow and pulse. But then one eyebrow twitches and he blinks.

"I'm not going to hurt your mum, Davey. We just want a bit of time together, that's all."

His voice is calm and controlled. He puts his hand in his pocket and pulls out a handful of coins. "Go on, take some. Go down the shops, treat yourself."

He's smiling at me, the stupid sod. As if I'd leave him alone with Mum. "Get lost," I snap.

He shrugs. "Please yourself." He puts the money back in his pocket and pats Mum's shoulder. "Come on, Ali."

She lets him lead her up the stairs, doesn't even try to get away. But then she wouldn't, would she?

The bedroom door slams shut. I take a running kick at the sofa and gasp as I stub my toes. You weakling, you puny little shitfaced turd. He's got her and you did nothing to stop him.

9

*

Tell us what happened, David. Did your dad call to see you? Was your dad at home when your mum hurt herself? Did he hurt you? You don't need to say anything, just raise your hand if your dad was there.

I'm not raising my hand, it wasn't my dad that was there. I'll never call that murdering sod Dad. I'm going to get Him – hunt Him, track Him down – he can't imagine what he's got coming to Him.

two

Apart from a broken arm and a crack in my skull, I'm all right. I don't really need to be here in this crapshit hospital. I'm free to go whenever I want. They've even got a new family to look after me. Great, eh?

I'm on the bottom step, listening. I don't want to think about what's happening upstairs but I can't help it. I remember all the times he's hurt her, black eyes, bruised face. I can't let it happen again. I wish there was someone who'd help. At the shelter they called the police but we haven't got a phone and I daren't leave the house, I have to stay near Mum.

It's gone quiet. I can't hear anything. Gently, carefully I climb the stairs and put my ear to the bedroom door. He grunts, says something in a low, deep voice. I wait for Mum to answer so I know she's OK but she doesn't. I've got to see. My heart thumps as I put my hand on the doorknob. I'm just about to give it a shove when I hear Mum whisper; it's faint but she's not sobbing or panicking, she sounds OK. I wait another minute, hear him moan and mutter. It's horrible. I don't want to listen no more, don't want to think what he's up to.

Slowly, I retrace my steps, sliding noiselessly down the stairs. I hope he'll go soon. I wish he'd never found us, I wish I was bigger and stronger, wish I could throw him out.

My drawing book lies open on the table. Idly I flick through it – motorbikes and flowers, a fantasy landscape with a castle, giant triffids, the cat next door. Without thinking, I pick up a pencil and sketch – sharp cheekbones, two almonds for eyes, long eyelashes and above them, eyebrows that are smooth dark crescents; a long bony nose and strong, square jaw. An exact likeness of the face women go for; a poncy French footballer or ageing rock star. I shade in the dark curls, the frown lines on the forehead, and the image is so good that I'm mesmerized. I stare down at the paper and the man stares back at me. I've never got anybody so right before. It's Him.

My breathing quickens and my throat goes dry. The pencil zigzags across his face, random dark lines scrubbing him out, shading his eyes black, scribbling over his hair. I tear out the sheet of paper, screw it up and throw the pieces across the room. Then I go back to the stairs, sit down and wait.

At last I hear footsteps and down he comes, grinning like a scud who's nicked a burglar.

"You all right, Davey?" he asks as he buttons his shirt. "Your mum'll be down in a minute."

I scowl. He steps past and stands in front of me.

"We should have a chat, you and me. Haven't had much chance to see you lately but I'm going to be around a lot more now. We'll get things sorted, your mum and me."

I stand up. "You got to keep away, the court said. You shouldn't be here."

He grabs my wrist. "I'm your dad, Davey, and don't you forget that."

I grit my teeth and stare at him. "I'll call the scuds. They'll come and get you."

He shakes me loose. "You do that and see what you get."

His eyes are fierce, his hair's sticking out at one side and on his cheek there's a fresh deep scratch. Mum! I push past him and run up the stairs.

"Mum, you all right?"

She's sitting on the edge of the bed, head down, softly crying.

"I'm all right, David," she sniffs. "Don't worry."

My eyes dart over her but I can't see no injuries, he hasn't hurt her. I heave a sigh of relief. "Will he go now?"

"I hope so Davey, I hope so."

She puts her arm round me and gives me a hug. Her

hair falls over my face and it smells warm and lemony. The door creaks. He's come into the room and he's standing watching us.

He smiles, all smarmy, and walks over to the bed. "What's up with you two? You look like somebody's died. You oughta be happy. We're a family again, eh?"

Mum wipes her eyes. "It's been a shock, Martin, that's all. I haven't seen you for more than a year."

He sits down. "And who's fault's that, eh?" He puts his arm round her, then leans over to me and runs his hand over my bristly hair. "Glad to have your dad back, Davey, aren't you?"

I push his hand away. "No, I'm not glad. We don't want you. I want you to go, Mum wants you to go."

I might as well have plugged him into an electric socket. His jaw starts to judder and he hisses from between rigid teeth; any second he'll explode.

Mum puts her arm out, protectively. "He doesn't mean it, Martin. It's just going to take him time to get used to you being here again."

His fist comes up. "Doesn't mean it? He only threatened to call the police, jealous little bugger."

"He wouldn't do that. He was joking." Mum tries to laugh but what comes out sounds more like a strangled cry. She coughs. "Tell you what, let's have a cup of tea. You stay there, Mart. Me and David will make you a nice cup of tea. Come on, David, let's see if we can find some of those biscuits you like."

14

She gets up, pulling me to my feet. Everything would have been all right if I hadn't opened my big mouth. We could have gone downstairs, left him up there scratching his arse. We could have escaped. But I'm thick aren't I? I had to say it. "What biscuits?"

Mum throws me a warning look and he's on to it right away.

"What's going on? What you two cooking up?"

"Nothing, Martin."

He jumps up, stands in front of us. "You're going to do a runner, like you did before, aren't you? Saw me coming and cleared out."

"No, Martin, no."

Mum's voice is shrill. She gets hold of me and rushes me out the room. We're on the landing when he grabs her.

"Oh no, you don't. You're staying with me, Ali. He can make the tea and bring it up to us."

I'm livid with rage. Who does he think he is to come back ordering us about? He shouldn't even be here. I run at him and give him a push. "Clear off, leave us alone. We don't want you."

He grabs me, twists my arm, then with a mighty shove, slams me against the wall. The back of my head explodes. I stagger forwards, bash my forehead on his knee and fall heavily on my arm. I hear a crack, pain shudders through me. I lie for a moment, breathless and sick but I'm too mad to care. Somehow, I get to my feet and run at him again. He puts his hand up to hit me but Mum catches his arm.

"No, Martin, you've hurt him!"

He's shouting and trying to get me but Mum's pulling him back, so he turns and slaps her face – a hard stinging slap that sends her reeling. She gives a shrill cry as she totters backwards. Her foot misses the top step, her hand claws for the rail, then – she falls.

I run forward but there's nothing I can do. She seems to be falling in slow-motion, her blue dress billowing like a parachute. Her back touches a step, she rolls, twists sideways then her head hits the ground. *Thwack!* A dull thud like snow falling off a roof. *Thoop*. A sound that's hard and soft at the same time. *Flump* – a pumpkin splitting open. She doesn't make a sound but lies still as stone, her quiet filling up all the space.

I can't move. I'm sucked in by a giant wave that tosses me over and knocks me down, my stomach full of squirming, foaming, squelchy bile. I hold on to the banister, gasping and heaving. Vaguely I'm aware of him clattering down the stairs making weird whimpering noises.

I want to scream but I can't. All the breath is squeezed out of me, my throat tight and hot and burning like I've run a hundred metres. Lights flash in my head, my vision blurs. I blink and swallow. I see him looking down at Mum then up at me. His mouth hangs open, his eyes are wide and startled, his shoulders sag, hands dangle useless as old boxing gloves. Then, he collapses on the step and starts to cry.

If it hadn't been for Mum lying there I'd have laughed out loud, happy that he was scared shitless. But Mum's body is all crooked and wrong and she hasn't moved.

Hanging on to the rail, I feel my way down the steps, push past him and crawl to Mum. She's white, pale as milk; her eyes are staring but she isn't seeing and there's a bubble at the corner of her mouth. When it pops it leaves a red stain.

I kneel down beside her and whisper her name but she doesn't move. Then he comes over blubbering like a baby, tears streaming down his face as he leans over and shakes her.

"No, Ali. Oh no."

He falls on her, arms and legs scrabbling about as if he's trying to swim and he howls like a mad dog.

"Forgive me, Ali, forgive me."

I kick him hard. "Leave her alone."

He straightens up and grabs me, pushing his face right into mine.

"It was an accident, an accident. I was never here. You understand? You never saw me."

His eyes are wide and frightened as a nightmare. For a moment we stare at each other then he runs for the door. I hear it open, the gate clangs, the car engine starts up and he blasts off up the street.

Relief rushes through me. Now I can make Mum better, just like all the times before. I'll bathe her head, put ice on her bruises. I needn't worry, she'll be OK.

Her eyelids flutter and she gives a gentle moan. I knew she was just pretending, waiting till he cleared off.

"Mum, wake up. He's gone. You can open your eyes now. It's all right, honest, he won't come back. Come on, you don't have to lie on this cold floor. I'll get you on to a chair."

My arm's singing with pain, yelling to be heard. It's hard for me to move but I put one arm round her and try to lift her up. Can't do it, I hurt all over and everything's tipping sideways.

"I'm sorry, Mum. I can't lift you. Don't worry, we'll just lie here, we'll be all right, he won't come back."

Blood's trickling from the back of her head. I should get a scarf or something, try and stop it. I should get a blanket to keep her warm. I lean on my good arm, try to stand up but everything starts swimming. The banister rail's slippery as a fish, my hand slips and I bang my knee as I hit the floor. It all goes black and I slide away, slip down into a deep hole.

When I wake it's dark. Everything's furry round the edges. I can't move. My toes and fingers are numb with cold. I'm frozen as a fishfinger, frozen into a solid stick, 'cept my knees are bent. If somebody wanted to move me they'd have to thaw me out first. My fingers are stiff as I reach out and touch Mum's face. She's cold too, cold as ice.

Outside everything's quiet. Nobody slamming doors, no kids shouting, everybody in bed. I hear a car – not his, a smooth sound, *thrum, thrum*. He won't come back, will he? Clang, a dustbin rattles. Creak, the back door. Is it him? Is he outside? I listen so hard my ears tingle but I can't hear nothing more, only silence, growing, expanding, buzzing loud as a cloud of flies, making my head throb – hurt bad.

I'm sorry, Mum. I tried, I tried to stop him but he was too strong. Great hulking brute. Bloody bastard. You shouldn't have let him in Mum, you shouldn't have.

So, you're not going to talk to me, David?

I look up and see her green eyes sparkling like jelly tots.

But you can hear me, can't you? I do want to help you. You're feeling sad and sorry about your mum, I know that. But none of it was your fault, David. You must believe that.

My fault? Was it my fault? I didn't choose a cruel, raving maniac for a father. I didn't let him into the house. I didn't push Mum down the stairs. There's only one person that's to blame – Him, Martin Dawson, and when I get out of here I'm going to get Him. I owe Mum that.

three

"David. I'm so glad to meet you."

She holds the door open.

"I'm Jill Robinson. Come in."

Blue grey eyes; fuzzy brown hair; smiling mouth; red shirt; bracelets that jangle as she puts out her hand. I pull back but Miss Social Worker is right behind me and pushes me forwards. I avoid shaking hands with Jill Robinson but trip on the step and drop my bag.

"Oh dear, are you all right?" Jill asks. She picks up the bag. "Here let me. Shall we take it straight to your room?" I look down; see red sandals peeping from under a long dark skirt, the sandals turn and step away from me, the long skirt swishes.

"Come on, follow me," she says.

There's red carpet on the stairs, yellow walls and lots of pictures. Some are kids' drawings that have been framed, some are big abstract daubs of colour and then

20

there's photos – lots of heads with smiles – it's like a ruddy picture gallery. I follow the long sweeping skirt over a wide landing, past a row of doors.

"Here we are," Jill Robinson says.

There's a sticker on the door. It says my name in silver-blue letters. DAVID'S ROOM.

I suppose I'm meant to go inside, so I open the door. It's small, not much floor space between the furniture, but it'll do me, I won't be here long. Everything matches. Blue and white curtains, blue striped cover on the bed, blue pillows and blue flowered cushions. There's a desk with blue cupboard doors and on the walls there's some big posters – rock bands and a snowboarder flying against a blue sky. An old teddy bear sits on the desk. He isn't blue, he's yellow and has one eye.

"Make yourself at home," Jill Robinson says.

It doesn't feel like home. It feels like I'm in somebody else's bedroom. I turn round thinking I'd like to leave but Jill is right behind me, smiling, happy as a birthday card.

"There," she says, putting my bag on the bed. "You can unpack when you want."

The bag isn't heavy. I didn't want none of my old stuff – just what they got me. Nothing to remind me. No jumpers with name tags or trousers with the hems stitched up. I got new things now – boxer shorts, pyjamas, baggy jeans. Miss Social Worker asked me what football team I supported; said she'd buy clothes in my favourite team colours. Daft bitch. As if I cared. Football's shite. He likes football.

I look at my bag and see the name tag. DAVID DAWSON. I'm like a ruddy evacuee.

From the doorway Miss Social Worker coughs. I turn to look at her. She's hovering near the door as if her shoes are muddy and she daren't step on the carpet.

"Well, I'll be going," she says. "Leave David to get to know everybody. I'll see myself out."

She smiles her social-worker smile before she disappears and I can tell she's glad to go. I'd be happy to stick a rocket up her bum to help her on her way. She's an idiot. Get to know everybody. There's only two people as far as I can see – Mr and Mrs Robinson, Jill and Eric, and I've already met one of them.

I hear her tapping down the stairs. The front door slams. Good riddance. Thank God she's gone. Stupid bitch! I hope I never see her again. Her car starts up, the last connection to my old life, disappearing down the road in dust, just like He roared away that afternoon. Now I'm a new person. An orphan. No Mum. No Dad.

Jill leaves me to "settle in". She tells me where the bathroom is and says she's going to make a cup of tea. She'll have it ready in the kitchen in a few minutes. The kitchen's at the back to the right of the stairs.

She closes the door behind her and I sit on the bed.

It's soft and springy and smells clean – everything smells clean, it's like the bloody hospital.

I sit staring at the posters. The boy on the snowboard's dressed in all the right gear, poncy git. He's holding out his arms, zooming down the mountain, flirting up snow. Bet he's never had no problems. He wants to try my life for a balancing act. I'm all right as long as I don't think about Mum, don't think about her lying in that shiny coffin and what they done with her.

There's a dog barking downstairs – a door opens. I hear a man's voice, deep and firm. "Down, Griffy. Be quiet."

The dog barks again. Does it live here or is it just visiting? Nobody told me they had a dog – they would have told me if they had a dog, wouldn't they?

I go down into the kitchen and there's a black dog sitting, panting. It gets up and comes to me, leans against me pressing its nose into my thigh. When I try to push it away, it licks my hand.

"Oh, David. I hope you don't mind dogs," Jill says, then she laughs loudly. "Well, it's a bit too late now, I suppose. Anyway, it seems as if you're friends already. Griffy's everybody's friend, she loves people."

I wipe my hand on my trousers and back away. I don't love people and I don't need friends. I definitely don't need this dog prodding me with its paw, nuzzling its head into my crotch and looking up at me with soft brown eyes. I'm not stroking it, I'm not touching it and just to make sure, I clench my fingers tight.

A smallish bloke wearing glasses comes in. "Hallo, I'm Eric," he says, holding out his hand. I thrust my good hand behind my back and scowl.

"Hi, you must be David," he says. He gestures towards the dog. "Is she being a nuisance? Come here, Griffy!" He bends down to stroke and tickle her. "She just wants some fuss," he says.

He seems a bit soft to me; cooing and talking in a high-pitched voice. "Who's a beautiful girl, then? Did you give David a nice welcome, did you?" The top of his head is nearly bald but around his ears and neck there's a fringe of light-brown hair. I'd shave it all off if I was him. What's the use of a scruffy bit round the edges? You might as well be bald.

"I've made some tea," Jill says. "Sit down. Do you want a cup, David?"

I don't answer. I'm not going to. After a while it doesn't matter if you speak or not. People tell you things, anyway.

We're doing another X-ray.

You're getting better. You'll soon be out of here.

The Robinsons are very nice. You'll like them.

The funeral is next Monday.

No need for talk. People take care of me, give me what they think I want and that's OK by me. All I need to do is work on my plan. Plan A – to track, to hunt, to kill. Like he always said, *You've got to look out for number one in this life.* And that's what I'm doing, looking out for number one – Him. He's my number-one target and sooner or later, I'll find Him.

Jill pours me a cup of tea just in case I want one and I spoon in two sugars like Mum used to. I watch the tea whirling round and round and remember Mum warming her hands, humming – no, I won't think.

"There's skiing on the telly or some old film but we could watch *The Simpsons* later. Do you like *The Simpsons*?" Eric asks.

It doesn't matter, they'll switch it on. Not many people can stand silence. I don't mind it, except that sometimes I can't stop myself thinking. I try to remember Mum happy, her eyes dancing, the way she'd look when I did something nice for her, made her a cuppa or got her a good book from the library. But I can't think about her for long or I start seeing her lying on the floor, dead. That's when my head starts to buzz and everything I look at breaks into bursts of light – fireworks going off behind my eyes. Sometimes, at the hospital, they gave me a tablet to help me sleep. I wish I had some of them now, a big bottle so I could pop a few in and pull the switch when everything got too bad. But I can't switch off for long because I have to get Him.

The kitchen is hot. I'm sweating in my anorak. They must have put a lot of money in the meter. One time,

Mum and me lived in a flat where the meter was broken. We kept putting the same pound coin through. We were warm as cats and we had lights and electric for cooking and the telly on and everything.

"Why don't you take your coat off, David?"

See, people know what you're thinking even when you say nothing. I stand up and pull off my anorak.

Jill takes it. "I'll put it in the cloakroom, just through the hall, door on the left. In fact, let's show you round the house then you'll know where everything is. And it won't be long before you're the one making the tea and taking Griffy for walks."

She laughs, a high tinkling sound like spoons in cups and she puts her hand on my arm. "Come on, we'll do a tour."

She gets up and I follow, obedient as the dog. She shows me where to hang my coat, then I follow her into what she calls the sitting room. It's bursting with rugs and cushions and sofas and stuff and there's books everywhere. I think she expects me to say something like "it's nice," because she stands looking at me but I don't give a toss. They could have put me in a bus shelter and it wouldn't have mattered. I'm not staying.

She turns and walks off. The dog stays with me. It doesn't need a tour, it's seen it all before. It leans its head against my leg but I pull my leg away and walk backwards till I bump into Jill.

"This is the dining room," she says.

Well, great, I've never had one of those before. I'm sure it'll improve the quality of my life no end. There's a big polished table crowned with a colourful bunch of flowers and next to it is a room she calls the "office". That's a lot of rooms for two people.

Upstairs, we pass Jill and Eric's room which she points at and then she stops at a door which has a big DO NOT DISTURB sign on it. Pushing down the handle, Jill lets the door swing back.

"Simon's room," she says. "It's a bit of a tip. He likes clutter, won't get rid of a thing." She steps aside so I can see the heaps of books and papers, mugs and beer mats. "Simon's at university but you'll probably meet him. He'll be back for Easter."

I doubt it, I won't be here.

She closes the door and heads down the corridor. "This is Charlotte's room," she says. Her voice sounds a bit funny like she's trying to swallow at the same time as speak. She coughs and when she speaks again it sounds more normal. "Charlotte died just over two years ago," she says. "In an accident. We miss her very much."

Her face has lost its birthday-card smile. "I don't come in here very often," she says, opening the door. "But I want to show you so there's no mystery."

Mystery? It's no mystery to me. When you're dead, you're dead. That's it. Gone.

I want to tell her that she needn't show me the room

if it upsets her but I don't say anything. She walks in and I follow. It's very bright, the colours are like Smarties and there's a big window letting in lots of light.

Jill picks up a photograph in a frame and holds it out. "Look, this is Charlotte," she says.

Just as I step forward, Griffy squeezes past me and jumps on to the bed, snuggling down on the yellow duvet.

Jill purses her lips. "They say dogs forget people after six months," she says. "But I'm not so sure. Griffy was Charlotte's puppy."

I look at the photo of a girl with blonde hair. The girl is about the same age as me, she's pretty. I want to say she looks nice and I'm sorry she died but I don't. Words aren't no use anyway, I know that.

Jill puts the photo back on the bedside table. The room's full of stuff that must have belonged to Charlotte. Guitar, dance shoes, hockey stick, roller blades. It's no good now, so why don't they sell it?

When we get back to the kitchen, Eric's cooking. He's chopping onions and making the place stink. "Creating a curry," he calls it.

He asks Jill to pass him some spices. She reaches for a rack of little jars, places them on the counter beside him, then she opens rows of cupboard doors to show me where things are kept. There's tins and tins, and packets of food stacked in rows like at the supermarket;

tonnes of stuff – they could open a shop – it would feed me and Mum for a year.

The damned dog is nuzzling at me again. I move aside and stick my hand firmly in my pocket. Jill comes over and pats her. "She's a bit persistent, isn't she? I'll tell you what, would you like to take her to the park – give her a walk?"

"Yeah, that's a good idea," Eric says. "Give me some space. I need to concentrate."

Jill rolls her eyes. "Hmm, I wonder how I ever managed to cook anything when I had two children round my feet?"

Eric laughs but I turn away. How can they laugh? Charlotte's not round anybody's feet no more. She's dead.

Jill goes to get our coats. "Come on, we'll leave him to it," she says. "Griffy, walk!"

The dog's ears prick up at the word "walk". She wags her tail then dashes to pick up a red ball. I struggle with my anorak, pushing my good arm into the sleeve then trying to loop the rest of it around my back and shoulder so that it covers the pot on my other arm. When I'm ready Jill clips a lead on to the dog.

"Here, you take her. She'll pull but tell her firmly to walk to heel."

Fat chance! As soon as Jill opens the door, the stupid dog throws herself forward and we catapult out the house like greyhounds out of traps. I just about manage to hang on as it charges for the gate.

"She's stronger than she looks, isn't she?" Jill says when she catches up.

Like a bloody tiger, I think, my fingers are tingling. Jill unlatches the gate, then at full tilt we're through and into the street.

"Tell her to heel," Jill shouts.

I wrap more of the lead round my hand, trying to yank it back, then I manage to pull the ruddy thing to a halt. It sits down, panting, while we wait for Jill to join us.

I look about me at the unfamiliar street. It's very tidy. There's no litter, and the cars parked at the kerb or in driveways are shiny and new with whole number plates, aerials and wing mirrors. Not rusty old painted-up bangers like his.

At the bottom of the street we cross the road and go through giant-sized black and gold gates. Beyond is a wide stretch of open grass. Griffy stops and drops the ball.

"She wants you to throw it," Jill says.

The ball's soggy with spit. I don't want to touch it, never mind throw it, but I suppose it's one way to pass the time. I unclip the lead, and, with my good arm, throw the ball as far as I can. It flies in a wide arc, red against the light-blue sky. Catch that if you can. She does! She's like lightning, dashing, leaping and catching the ball before it touches the ground. She's amazing, clever as a circus dog. Then she hurtles back and drops the ball at my feet.

"Fast, isn't she?" Jill says.

The dog's eager, ready for the next throw, ears pricked up, one paw raised. I throw the ball again and again. With the sharp breeze stinging my cheeks, I watch her jump and catch, circle round then come pelting back, narrowly missing my knees.

Jill's waving her arms about. "It's getting cold," she says. "Let's walk on. We'll go down to the river."

And suddenly I think, what river? And I realize I don't know where I am. I'm not sure which side of town we're on. It was a long ride from the hospital and Mum and me had only lived here for a few weeks. I swallow hard as Griffy circles my legs. If I don't know where I am, then how can I carry out my plan? Somehow I've got to get information. To track, to hunt, to kill – that's my mission. And I mustn't let anything stand in my way.

four

I'm watching telly when Griffy starts barking like mad and Jill comes into the sitting room.

"There's someone to see you, David."

She's talking gently, doesn't want to freak me out, but spidery fingers are creeping up and down my back, jarring my nerves, making me tremble.

Griffy is jumping and sniffing at the two visitors hovering in the hall. She's excited, curious, she doesn't know who they are but I do. I could tell her – scuds. I knew they'd come sooner or later. Not that I've got anything against them, they've helped me and Mum out many a time. But I'm nervous, I don't want them poking their noses in, I want to sort things out myself.

"They just want to ask you a few questions, David. Is that all right?"

I don't answer and I don't move. I sit on the sofa in front of the telly and watch the Wheel of Fortune spinning round. Eight hundred pounds, give us a "T".

"Down, Griffy," Jill commands, as the scuds slope into the room.

I know they'll ask their questions with or without permission. It's their job. On the screen the next letter is "S". The catchphrase is SITTING DUCK – any idiot can see that but the contestants can't. One of the visitors says my name. Now I'm the sitting duck.

Detective Sergeant Gardner and Detective Constable Perrins introduce themselves and come to stand in front of me. They're both in plain clothes – very plain. Gardner's suit is grey and Perrins is wearing black jeans and a dark anorak. Gardner sidesteps to stand in front of the screen.

Griffy eyes the scuds suspiciously then trots over and lies near my feet. I don't mind, at least somebody's on my side.

Jill switches off the TV and invites the scuds to sit down. Gardner chooses the armchair nearest to me. Her grey suit has a very short skirt and as she crosses her legs I catch a flash of thigh. Embarrassed, I swing my eyes up to her face. Her hair is blonde, not gold blonde like Mum's, but pale, it's tied back in a ponytail.

"How are you feeling, David?" Her voice is soft. When I don't answer she waits for a while, not fidgeting or anything but just looking at me. "I know it must be very difficult for you without your mum," she says.

I avoid her eyes and stare down at Griffy.

"My mum died when I was fifteen and I remember how lonely I felt," she says.

I suppose she tells me this so I'll think we've got something in common. When I don't say anything she leans forward and clasps her hands round her knees. I can tell she's trying to get me to look at her.

"We're here because we want to find out how your mum died," she says. "We want you to tell us what you can remember."

When she stops speaking she sits perfectly still. Her knees shimmer in the light of the gas fire. Perrins's anorak rustles and I can feel him waiting for me to speak. But I don't want to tell them what I remember, I don't want to remember, full stop. I don't want to think about anything that happened that afternoon. I try not to think about it because if I do, it does my head in. I think I should have done more to help Mum, I think I should have found somebody to help us or rung for the ambulance. I think I shouldn't have made Him angry. I think if I'd been stronger then Mum wouldn't have died.

In the middle of the night I imagine if I hadn't done this, if I hadn't said that, if I'd stopped him pushing Mum, if I'd held on to his arm, if I'd. . . If, if, if. Enough ifs to make me bite my cheek and screw up my eyes till my head aches. Enough ifs to send me jumping out the window and falling *splat* to the ground.

Gardner sniffs and reaches in her pocket for a tissue. She's wearing perfume. It smells like flowers and a picture comes into my head. Mum wearing a bright-pink dress she bought at Oxfam – dead pleased with it she was. She tried it on and it fit her real nice and she danced in the kitchen, danced to Radio One.

I swallow hard and bend down, pretending that I'm really interested in stroking the dog. The dog thinks I'm interested too and lays her head on my knee. She's panting – it's hot in this room, hot and stuffy. The air's heavy. They're waiting for me to speak. They'll have to wait a long time. They'll ask me another question in a minute. Nobody can stand this much silence. Jill looks at me, her mouth zipped tight. She's letting the scuds sort this one out.

"We think your dad was in the house when your mum died. Is that right?"

Fluffy bits of hair have escaped from Gardner's ponytail and they waft about in the heat. She waits for me to answer and when I don't, her voice is a bit louder when she speaks again. "I'm sure you want everybody to know the truth about how your mum died, David, don't you?"

Too right, I do. I want the whole bloody world to know what an evil bastard he is. I want Him to be on telly, shown on the six o'clock news being bundled out of a police van with a blanket over his head. People pushing forward to get at Him, others throwing eggs and booing. I want everyone to know that he murdered my lovely, beautiful Mum. But they won't hurt Him enough. They won't kill Him. They don't have the death penalty no more. You have to live in Florida or Texas or somewhere hot for that.

"I know it must be difficult for you to think about it, David," Gardner says, "but any information at all would help – and talking about it might help you."

She sits sideways, wipes her nose, puts the tissue back in her pocket then twists her fingers, locking and unlocking them. She waits. I pat the dog again.

After a while she gives up waiting. "I remember after my mum died," she says. "I couldn't talk about it, I just couldn't. It was like I had this tight parcel knotted up inside me and if I started to unwrap it then I'd break apart and there was a bit of me that wanted to keep that parcel, all tight and unopened because then it was mine and I didn't have to share it."

I don't want to know about parcels. She's not going to win me over with that one. I prepare to give her one of my drop-dead glares but then I notice her eyes are blue, bright blue like Mum's – I hadn't expected that, so I blink and she carries on.

"It was too much to carry that parcel around all the time," she says. "I had to unwrap it or I would have gone mad."

She leans forward until her knees are nearly touching mine. Her voice is soft again. "David, please answer some questions. If you help us understand, you will help yourself – trust me, I know it's true."

I look away. Perrins is fidgeting. He clears his throat. I can tell he thinks it's going too slowly, he's impatient, wants to jump in, blast me with questions, wrestle my arm up my back and make me talk.

"We think your dad was at the house on the day your mum died, David. Is that right?" he asks.

I close my eyes and say nothing. Jill sighs. I expect she must be fed up, I've lived here for two days and I haven't spoken yet.

I look at the scuds and wonder if they've talked to Him. If they know where he is, and then Perrins answers my question.

"We'd ask your dad what happened if we could, but he's disappeared. We can't find him, David. We can't find him anywhere. Will you help us find him?" His tone is hard and anxious. "Don't you want to help us find your dad?" he asks, his voice rising sharply on the last word.

I take a deep breath and clench my fist. *Don't call Him my dad. He's not my dad. Don't call Him my dad, he's Him, just Him.*

I shout it inside my head but I don't say the words out loud. I look at Perrins as if I could tear his throat out. Then, I start to cry. It comes from nowhere, takes me by surprise. Big welling, bubbling sobs; I can't stop them.

I'd promised myself I wouldn't cry and I hadn't. Not even at the funeral, not when I saw Mum's friends from the shelter, not when I saw the coffin. I pictured Mum lying inside and I wanted to run to her and tell her not to go away but I kept myself controlled and instead I promised her – Mum, I won't shed no tears, I won't cry till I've found Him. And when I find Him, I'm going to smash his stupid head in and I'm going to say to Him this is for my mum because you killed her.

I'm furious that I'm crying now. I bite my lip and sniff hard. Jill puts her hand on my shoulder but I shake it off.

"I think you should go," I hear her say to the scuds. "It's early days, he's been through a lot."

Gardner replies quietly and I strain to hear what she says. It could be important.

"Obviously we want to interview the father. If he tries to get in touch let us know immediately. He's had little contact with David but I have a hunch he may want to get in touch now. Any information as to his whereabouts, clues . . . relatives . . . responsibilities . . . tragic . . . officers searching."

If I wasn't blubbing so much, I could hear better, but I think I got it. See? I don't have to talk. I've found out all I need to know.

Gardner stands over me, giving my arm the slightest touch. "We're going now, David. I'm sorry you're upset. We'll talk some more when you're feeling better."

38

I turn away and bury my head in the sofa. *Leave me alone, just leave me alone.* But the bloody dog jumps up, whimpering and pawing at my shoulder. *Go away, go away.* I push her hard but she doesn't budge, she's stubborn as shit. She dives under my armpit, rubbing her head on my chest and nuzzling her nose into my neck. One paw drops over my shoulder as if she's hugging me. *Stupid animal. Go away.* She taps me gently with her paw then whimpers again as if to comfort me. I bite my lip, clench my fist and sigh, then I lean forward and wrap my arm around her.

She's soft and warm and I sob into her thick black coat. It's like the dam's burst. I can't stop crying. All the stuff about Mum comes flooding into my head. I see her face, hear her voice. She's so real, it's like she's really with me, touching me, holding me, right beside me so I can smell the warmth of her. I hold on to Griffy because she's all I've got. I feel so bad I want to die. I wish I could just stop breathing and fall asleep for ever.

The front door slams, jolting me out of my misery. They've gone – off to try and find out where he's holed up. I sit up, blink hard and breathe deeply. No time for tears. If I sit around crying then I'll never do anything, I'll never work out a good plan. If I'm going to get Him for what he did to Mum then I've got to be calm and cunning and clever.

I gulp and swallow. I'm glad about one thing. They don't know where he is. They haven't got a clue. So, that puts me one up on them. I push the dog away. I've got to be tough. I can't afford to let anybody or anything get to me.

When Jill comes back Griffy's lying on the rug and I'm sitting quietly, staring into the fire.

"I'm sorry, David," she says. "I should have warned you. I didn't think they'd be here so soon. I asked them to give you a few days to settle in. I know it's hard for you. What you've gone through, nobody should have to endure."

She sits down beside me, doesn't say anything else, just sits staring into space like me. Then she clears her throat and finally she asks me, "Is it that you don't want to remember?"

I turn away, biting my lip. Then, I stand up and walk to the door. I need to be alone, I have to think.

five

I pull the door tight shut then jump on to the bed and slam my head back on the pillow. Damn the stupid police. Gardner with her pretty eyes and pretend sympathy and Perrins foaming at the mouth because I won't say nothing. As if I'm going to help them. I don't want him locked up. I want to find him. I want to stand over him with a knife pressed against his throat, the blade scoring his skin so that he's begging for mercy. Then I want to see his skin slit open and all the blood pour out – just like Mum's.

But, the difference is, he's asked for it, he deserves it. He's got it coming. Mum never hurt nobody. She was kind and gentle, careful not to upset him, never did nothing that would make him angry; tiptoed about like a mouse when he was around. He didn't deserve her, treated her like dirt. Bully, mean vicious bully.

I close my eyes and imagine he's my prisoner, tied to

a chair. I'm lighting a cigarette, pressing it down on to his bare skin. Sizzle, sizzle, the hairs on his arm scorch, then his flesh smoulders. His screams don't bother me, I show no mercy. I carry on pressing and pressing the lit fag into his arm until there's a big raw wound and a smell of charred flesh. Bastard, bastard, bastard!

I watch as his features crumple and crease and twist and his mouth roars. He squirms and writhes but still I torture him. "This is for Mum, this is for my mum," I say as I smash my fist into his nose.

David, David, a voice says gently. *David, please, please stop.*

I sit up and cover my ears.

David, if you torture him then you're no better than he is.

I shake my head to get rid of the voice. No, Mum no. I'm not listening. I won't listen to you or Jill or the scuds – not till I've killed him.

I roll from side to side biting the duvet, trying to blot out Mum's voice. I've got to be strong and calm, think clearly, make a plan, a proper plan. I lie for a moment clenching my fists and taking deep breaths then I sit up, open my eyes and think.

When I set my mind to it, I can think good. I'm not clever, can't read or write perfect, missed too much school, but I'm not stupid. I know it will be tough to track him down, I'll have to be sharp, sharper than the scuds. I'll need to think up a good plan, make a list of contacts and places he might be hiding. I've got the advantage because I know him better than they do and I can concentrate all my time and effort on finding him.

Suddenly I'm filled with energy. I swing off the bed, go over to the desk and pull out the biggest sheet of paper I can find.

Dear He-man, You broke the wrong arm – tough luck – I can still write. And, guess what? I'm coming to get you.

I don't write that – if I warn him – he might escape. Instead I pick up a red felt tip and make a big heading:

Target – Martin Dawson

Davids plan

Clues

Gran   Aunty Sue

It's a long time since I saw Gran (His mum) and Aunty Sue (His sister), haven't seen them since Mum and me left Derby. I remember the name of Gran's road, Pilot Street. I write that down and underneath I put any other clues I can think of.

best mate – Steve Forbert

Favorite Pub – White lion

Football team – Derby County The Rams

job –?

My head buzzes as I try to remember what I heard him tell Mum. He said he had a job in Derby selling double glazing and conservatories but I can't remember who he said he worked for so I write:

job – sellings things inshurence windows

I write insurance cos that's what he used to do but I don't write conservatories cos I can't spell it.

I try to think of other things that might help me find him – his hobbies and stuff like that, but I can't write no more, the letters are going fuzzy round the edges. I don't know if it's because of my concussion or that I don't sleep proper but I get these dizzy spells if I try and concentrate.

I slump down in the chair, rest my head on the desk and close my eyes. I try to picture Mum's face but it won't come. I wish she was here with me – she'd put her arm round me, say something nice, make me a hot drink. But then I tell myself not to be so daft, if Mum was here I wouldn't be doing this, would I? I wouldn't be sitting in a stranger's house making plans to kill somebody.

A sharp knock on the bedroom door makes me jump. Jill's voice comes through the woodwork, "David, are you all right?"

I stay still, my head leaning on the desk. If I don't move or speak perhaps she'll go away.

"David, can I come in?"

After a few moments the door handle rattles. Jill swishes into the room and stands behind me.

"I thought you might like some hot chocolate."

The floorboards creak as she moves then there's a sharp vibration under my cheek and I can tell she's put a mug down on the desk. She touches me lightly on the shoulder, "Don't let it go cold."

She's standing close to me, hovering, and I hope she can't see none of my writing because I don't want her nosing into my affairs. She's put the drink down, so why doesn't she go?

But she doesn't go, instead she speaks, her voice a bit quivery like she's nervous. "David. I've. . . I've got something for you," she says. "There's a parcel of your mum's things. You might not feel ready to look at them yet but they were given to me and I think it's only right that you should have them."

She pauses. I want her to go. I don't want her in here and I don't want none of Mum's stuff, I can't touch it.

"You don't have to look, not till you're ready. I'll just put them here in the bottom drawer for safe keeping."

There's a rustle of paper and the sound of the drawer opening.

"I hope there'll be a time when they comfort you," she says.

I wince. Not a chance. What use are things?

I hear her close the drawer and move away. Next time she speaks she's put on a bright voice. "I've got to go to the library later. I thought you might like to come with me. We could make you a member so you could choose some books, yeah?" The door handle rattles. "All right, good," she says. "I'll call you when I'm ready to go."

The door closes and her footsteps retreat. I lift my head and grip the desk. I don't want to look down, I don't want to catch the tiniest glimpse, I don't want to see a sliver of that parcel. Leaning back in the chair I swing my foot round and kick the drawer tight shut. No memories can escape now. I bang my fist down hard on the desk top. I don't want to think about what's in there – Mum's red purse, the little silver ring I gave her for her birthday, that necklace with the blue stone, her hair brush.

I screw my eyes up so I won't see her face, then I panic because I can't see it. I try to form a picture but it won't come. Panic swirls through my head and my stomach heaves. I can't remember what she looks like! I slam my fist into the desk again. She's gone, gone for ever.

My stomach goes all weird, sloshing around like it's part of the ocean. I'm shivering like I'm cold and when I get up my legs feel like jelly. I stagger across to the bed, collapse on to the mattress and curl up into a ball. Why doesn't everybody just leave me alone? I don't want Mum's stuff, none of it. I want her. I want Mum to be here – not stuff. I can't have any of it in my room, I can't. I got to get rid of it.

Before I know it I'm kneeling in front of the drawer, pulling it open. I lift out a big envelope and clutch it to my chest. I feel dizzy and weak and I'm breathing hard. I look down at the brown paper and see Mum's name – ALISON DAWSON – written across it. I can't stand it. Struggling to my feet I lurch across to the window and fiddle with the catch. It won't open. I bang and push at the glass but it doesn't shift. I give up and lean against the wall, staring down at the parcel I've put on the window ledge. I'm trembling like a crazy person. I am crazy. What was I was going to do? Sling Mum's things out of the window into the garden? Fat lot of use that would be, Jill would just gather them up and bring them back. No, put it somewhere out of sight, somewhere I won't have to look at it.

There's a space on top of the wardrobe. I stand on tiptoe and fling the package as far as I can, right to the back so that it hits the wall. It lands with a thud and something flies out. It's there on the floor over by the bed, something small and shiny. When I bend closer I see it's one of Mum's hair slides, one that has a blue star on the end, one of her favourites. I stare at it for a moment until it seems to float above the blue carpet. A hand reaches for it and the slide is lifted until it settles on a strand of gold hair. I see Mum clearly, so clear. She's looking into a mirror, concentrating on pinning the slide in exactly the right spot; there's a small frown on her face and her lips are pouting. She turns and looks at me. I blink hard. Then, I step forward, raise my foot and smash the slide into the carpet.

The hot chocolate goes next. I swipe it off the desk. A stream of brown snakes across the room and the mug rolls under the bed. *Smash*, I knock the lamp over, the teddy bear flies towards the door, the blue cushions hit the carpet and I rip one apart with my shoe. When I've done that I kick the wastepaper bin so it crashes against the desk leg.

That's better. I hate this bloody room. I'd like to destroy everything in it, all the poxy blue matching shelves and cupboards and duvets and pillows. I'm getting out of here as soon as I can.

I'm blazing hot now, sweat running down my face, trickling down my back and my heart's flapping like a mad bird. I wait for Jill to come charging up the stairs. She'll go ballistic when she sees this mess. But there's no sound from below, not even Griffy racing upstairs. I listen hard. All I can hear is my own breath panting in and out. Perhaps I've scared her. Perhaps she's standing in the hall listening, too frightened to come up. Bet she thinks I'm a maniac like Dad – no, not Dad, Him!

I kick the bin again, drag the duvet on to the floor, pick up a pen and throw it at the snowboarding poster. The pen smacks against it but the glass doesn't crack. I wish it had, I wish the smarmy snowboarding kid had a crack right through his head. I stamp on the lampshade and grind the glass from the light bulb into the carpet. I'll show them. I'll show them all.

Suddenly, Jill's voice rises from the hall. "David, I'm off to the library. Are you coming?"

What is she, thick or something? Didn't she hear the noise? Doesn't she know I'm smashing the place up? I go to the door and peer down the landing.

She's standing near the top of the stairs wearing a stupid red hat that looks like a squashed tomato.

"You need to wrap up warm. It's quite a walk to the library," she says.

I stare at her, my face burning.

She comes up the last two steps and smiles, actually smiles! "We all need to let off steam sometimes," she says. "Don't worry, we'll fix it. Go and put a jumper on and I'll get your anorak."

She doesn't look angry, not even a flash of annoyance. I catch myself standing with my mouth hanging open then turn and go back to my room.

A jumper? Doesn't she know I can't wear jumpers, you can't wear jumpers with a pot arm. My feet crunch on some glass, I kick the duvet aside and open the wardrobe. There's a fleecy zip thing that Miss SW got me, but my fingers are trembling so much I can't get it off the hanger. I pull it off with my teeth and then with my good hand manage to drape it round my neck. That will have to do.

Right, breathe deeply, calm yourself and walk like a good little boy to the library. You could even choose some books if it makes her happy. Let her think she's won this one. What she doesn't know is, you're only going with her because you want to clock where this house is, what side of town you're on and to suss out the quickest route to the town centre. Before I go, I take a last look round the room and smile at the mess. Sod 'em all.

Griffy and Jill are waiting in the hall. Jill sticks my anorak on top of the fleece. A double whammy – I look like an American football player.

"You all right?" she asks.

I scowl at her but when she hands me the lead and we go out the back door, I almost dance. We have blast off – step one in my plan.

To my surprise Griffy doesn't pull me into the flower beds or race out into the street but walks calmly to wait at the gate.

"She knows it's library day," Jill laughs. "She's not too keen on this trip because she has to wait outside."

At the gate we turn up the street instead of down to the park and Griffy trots at my side like the best-trained dog in the world – she doesn't even stop to pee. By the time we turn the corner and go out on to the main road she's practically lagging behind.

It's a busy road and I can tell Griffy doesn't like it any more than I do. I'm not used to a lot of traffic. Mum and me, we didn't go far – the fewer people who saw us then the less chance He had of finding us. I don't mean we never went out; we weren't shut away like prisoners but we had to be careful. This busy road is a bit of a shock and I clutch Griffy's lead as we cross a garage forecourt.

"This is where I usually fill up with petrol," Jill says. "And that," she says pointing to a big supermarket, "is where we do our shopping. We could go there tomorrow if you want. You could pick out food you like, biscuits, cereals, snack type things, yes?"

Of course I don't answer but Jill doesn't give up. While we walk past the supermarket car park she talks about the sort of books I might like to get from the library or, she says, I could choose a video. I'm not really interested but my ears prick up when she points out where the buses stop. I make sure I remember that piece of information.

As we carry on downhill she points out the famous twisted spire of the church, the new sports centre and the bottom edge of the park. Then, when we're opposite a big roundabout she stops and shows me the road signs. Helpfully she points to each one – BAKEWELL, MANCHESTER, MATLOCK. Then she swings round and points to SHEFFIELD.

"Look, that's where you used to live, isn't it?" she asks.

But I'm only half listening because I've noticed another sign over the road. I look at it and feel a shiver of excitement. It's the one direction Jill's missed out. It reads: Derby – 26 miles.

six

I press my face into Griffy's thick coat. Her heart beat thumps against my ear – *thrum, thrum*.

"What about jotting some of your thoughts down on paper, David?"

Another question. She's been sitting opposite me all morning, asking, waiting, then answering herself. She's patient, I'll give her that. Perhaps they teach them that at social-worker school. Rule number one: keep your cool – even when the customers drive you barmy. I could tell her she's no need to bother with me, my bag's packed, I'm leaving.

I squint at her through Griffy's black fur. She's wearing black – black skirt, black jacket, black shoes. They should tell her to wear some bright colours, cheer herself up a bit. But then it must be a miserable kind of job, forever trying to sort out people's problems. I don't think her heart's in it. When she smiles it looks fake, even Griffy doesn't bother with her – one sniff and she's done.

Jill comes in with cups of tea. Milk, sugar? Miss Social Worker looks relieved. She turns to Jill and smiles. "I've just been suggesting to David that perhaps he might like to write things down, let us know how he's feeling."

She says it as if we've been having a cosy chat. Jill nods and agrees it's a good idea, she doesn't mention she's already suggested it.

I did start writing. It was a letter to Mum, a sort of goodbye letter. Jill told me that's what she did when Charlotte died cos she never got to say goodbye, but when I tried, it didn't work. I only got as far as, Dear Mum – then I started remembering too much.

Jill says it will take time, you can't rush grief. Miss Social Worker says I should see somebody who'll help me with my problems – a council person. I don't want to see nobody from the council. If they'd put us in a safe place he wouldn't have found us. Anyway I won't talk, so what's the use?

I close my eyes and stroke Griffy. She heaves a big sigh as she rests her head on my shoulder. The gas fire's warm, the teacups rattle and I do my best to join Griffy drifting off to sleep. Miss SW is talking about me going to school. I've heard it before and I don't want to know. I press my ear closer to Griffy's side trying to shut her out but the high whine of her voice gets through. She's asking Jill whether I'm eating and sleeping and if I'm having any other problems.

Jill doesn't say much. I wait for her to spill the beans about my wrecked room but she doesn't mention it. All she says is that I need time to "settle in". I go through my plan. First, get to Derby, then, find Gran's house. Turn up on the doorstep looking forlorn, give her some bullshit about my horrible foster home, say I want to live with Dad and ask where he is. Yeah, I reckon that'll work. How I'm actually going to top him I haven't worked out but it can't be that difficult – he managed it in seconds. I just wish I could get started, wish Miss Social Wanker would leave.

At last I hear the zip of a briefcase and she leans down to say goodbye. I keep my eyes shut until I hear her rustle to the door. Thank God she's gone. I hope it's the last I see of her. But she isn't done yet, I can hear her in the hall talking to Jill – she's dropped her voice to a whisper and that alerts me. I push Griffy aside, slip off the sofa and move closer.

They're round the corner standing in the middle of the hall. I close the door behind me hoping they'll think I'm on the other side. It works. Miss SW raises her voice.

"Can you manage him for another week? Of course, I'll call again to check everything's OK."

What does she mean "another week"? They said I could stay here. They put me here, she's been talking about me going to school. Jill said it was my home. She said I could stay. My name's on the friggin' bedroom door. I grip the doorframe, digging my nails into the paintwork. I hate the way they treat me like I'm some kind of parcel, put me here, send me there.

Jill's saying something I can't hear, something about me needing more time. When Miss SW answers I hear her loud and clear.

"If Dad turns up, we may have a problem. He might want David to live with him."

Dad? Who's Dad? That bastard – Him? I'm so angry I feel I could explode – go off *bang* like a firework! I step round the corner and stand in full view, shaking. If she's got something more to say she'd better know I'm listening. But neither she nor Jill can see me, they've moved to the front door and have their backs to me. Miss Faker carries on talking.

"If the police eliminate him from their inquiries, I don't know that we can refuse. There was an injunction to stop Mr Dawson contacting the boy's mother but as far as we know he's never harmed David."

"But David's injuries?"

Yes, what about my broken arm, bruises, concussion? Explain that, Miss Fake Social Worker.

She hesitates a split-second before answering. I see her hair swing as she shakes her head. "The report wasn't conclusive. The injuries to both mother and David could have resulted from a fall."

"But there's a history of past violence isn't there?" Jill asks.

Miss SW's voice is smooth as ice cream. "Well, yes. But it's difficult for us to do anything without real evidence."

I don't believe what I'm hearing – course there's real evidence. He put me in hospital and Mum's dead. And before that he battered her black and blue. Scuds got him one time when the neighbours phoned – took a knife off him. Mum was a regular at Casualty till she got smart and left him. What more evidence do they need? Are they blind – stupid, completely dense? The scuds are looking for him, they want to question him. Isn't that enough? They can't send me to live with him, they can't!

"David, what's the matter?"

I'm trembling, holding on to the back of the sofa. Jill puts a hand on my arm, shakes it gently, trying to get me to look at her, but I turn away.

"David, what is it?"

I tense my shoulders and my breath comes hot and quick.

"David, tell me why you're upset. I can't help you if I don't know what's wrong."

Her voice is breaking up, she's worried. I'm glad, I hope she feels rotten. She said I could stay here, I thought I could trust her but she's just like all the rest. I snort a long quivering breath down my nose.

Jill sighs. "Talk to me, David. Give me a chance. I want to understand."

I'm not listening to her pleas. I want to shout in her face, "You're stupid. You're all thick. Can't you see? He's a bloody murderer!"

I hold my breath to stop myself shouting, then I get dizzy. I lean against the sofa, closing my eyes. Faces loom behind my eyelids. Him, angry and stone sharp; Mum, scared and helpless, she's falling – her cry shoots like a spike through my brain. Blood's pouring from her head, oozing over the floor. It's the same nightmare whether I'm awake or asleep. I try to help her but I can't – my legs won't move. Everything blurs, my ears buzz and then the only thing I see is a signpost – Derby 26 miles.

I open my eyes and look at Jill. Her face is furrowed and anxious. I'd like to talk to her, explain about some of the things eating away at my brain but I know if I utter one word, everything will burst out – *pop*, like a cork from a bottle. And I'll drain away.

I brace my shoulders and give her a hard stare. She blinks and steps back as if I've hit her. I push past, rush into the hall and race up the stairs.

The door of my room slams behind me and I open a cupboard and drag out my sports bag. I'm going. I've got to. I'm not being handed over to him like a dog's dinner. I refuse to be in his power. That's not in my plan. I want to track him down, catch him by surprise, jump him from behind, get him when he's least expecting it and then – make him suffer. I don't care how long it takes or what I have to do, I'll find him.

I open the desk drawer, find the £5 note I got from the social and thrust it in my pocket. Then I reach for my fleece that's hanging in the wardrobe. When I step back I look up and for a moment my heart stops – I can't see the parcel I flung up there. It's gone. Putting my foot on the floor of the wardrobe I lever myself up and feel around. Right in the back corner my fingers touch the packet. I pull it out and see Mum's name's written on it like a headline. I want to drop it. I don't want to look at what's inside, don't even want to feel it but I can't leave it behind. Quickly I stuff the fleece in my bag and shove the package underneath.

There's a scraping at the door, Griffy wants to come in. I'm not sure what to do. I don't want her following me, I want to leave quickly and quietly, without anybody knowing.

When I open the door she bounces in and puts her paws on my knees. Don't go soft, don't stroke her, but I can't resist. She's looking up at me, like I'm the person she loves most in the whole world, her eyes so trusting. I touch her head, stroke her ears, then sigh and push her away. She watches while I zip up my bag; she knows I'm leaving.

I point to the bed. "Up, Griffy," I whisper. A treat she can't refuse. "Griffy, stay." I wait while she settles down. Then, when she's stretched out and relaxed, I pick up my bag and zoom out of the room. Closing the door gently behind me, I stop on the landing and listen. Jill's talking on the telephone somewhere beneath me. I slide noiselessly down the stairs and I'm away.

It's been a sunny day but the light's fading now and it's growing cold – not a good time to leave. I don't even want to think about where I'm going to spend the night.

I pull up the hood of my anorak and hurry past the petrol station and supermarket. At the roundabout I stop and wonder how I'm ever going to get to the other side. It's rush hour, there's no break in the traffic and I've got to cross six lanes to follow the sign – Derby 26 miles.

I wander along the kerb daring myself to step out. Waves of headlights wash over me. My head zings. I sway sideways, stumble and step back. There's an island in the middle of the road, if I judge it right I can make it there. I wait for ages, dangling on the kerb, then for a moment there's a lull and I wade through the pool of darkness, dash to the island and dart to the other side. I run towards the signpost and I'm on the right road – Derby 26 miles.

seven

I've only just stuck out my thumb when a car slows and pulls over. I hurry towards it, putting my bag down so I can open the door. A wave of warm air leaps out at me.

"Where're you going?"

A middle-aged bloke with gingery hair and bushy moustache leans across, one hand on the wheel.

"Derby," I say.

"Missed your bus have you? Hop in."

I climb in; pulling my bag after me. The man takes it and as he turns to put it on the back seat, his leather jacket rustles and billows up round his neck; he unzips it.

"What you done to your arm?"

"Broke it."

"I can see that. Can you manage your seat belt?"

"Yeah."

I fasten the seat belt and we move off. I'm dead

chuffed. The heater's blasting out, I'm warm, we're moving fast and I reckon we'll be in Derby in less than an hour.

"Anybody expecting you in Derby?" the man asks.

"Yeah, my dad."

The heat makes me feel sleepy and I begin to nod off, my head bouncing about so that every so often I jerk awake. The road to Derby isn't as straight as I thought it would be, we seem to be turning left and right, going up and downhill. I doze, lose track and only open my eyes when the car bumps and shudders to a halt.

"Just stopping for a snack. Been on the road all day."

The man puts the light on and reaches in the back for a flask. He hands me a cup to hold while he pours out coffee.

"Would you like some chocolate? I've got some KitKats in my bag."

I don't answer. I'm too busy looking out of the window trying to see where I am. There're some bushes in front of us but I can't see much else, it's all dark.

"Don't worry. I've just pulled off the road for a minute, felt sleepy myself. You were really gone there for a while. Go to sleep easily, do you?"

I don't answer.

He waves a KitKat. "Good job I picked you up," he says. "Young lad like you hitching a lift – never know who might stop. Some funny people about these days." He peels off the wrapper, sticks the bar under his moustache and takes a bite. "You want to be careful," he says.

His eyes are hypnotic, all the while he's munching and swallowing he's staring at me, his pupils drilling holes in my skull. I shift nervously in my seat, look away, then gently slide my hand down to unclick the seat belt.

He finishes the chocolate, licking at the bristly hairs hanging over the corners of his mouth, the foil wrapper rustles as he squeezes it into a ball. "Bet you like chocolate, don't you?" he asks. "I've got some more bars in my bag."

When he turns to root through his bag, I feel for the door catch. Too late! His hand touches the back of my neck. I freeze. His fingers snake upwards running over my hair. He chuckles.

"You crop your hair close, don't you? Think it makes you look tough, do you? You're not tough though, are you? I can tell that you're a nice lad." Gently, he tweaks my ear lobe. "Bet you wouldn't mind doing me a little favour, would you?"

I gulp as his hand strokes my ear, his leather jacket crackles as he leans closer. When his arm circles my shoulder, icy shivers run through me and I start to shake. I want to push the door open and make a run for it but I'm trembling so much I can't move. It seems unreal, as if it's not happening to me. I don't put up any resistance, letting him pull my head down on to his chest. His breath is hot on my neck, he begins to pant, then he arches his back and rises in his seat. He lets go of me, his fingers fumbling with his trousers. Pervert! I hear the word ring out as if I'd yelled it. Pervert!

When his hand comes up again I'm ready for him, I knock it away and his fingers smack back against the steering wheel. The flask falls off the dashboard spilling hot coffee over his knee. He jerks back, shouting.

"Ouch! What you playin' at?" He grabs a bunch of tissues, swiping at his trousers. "You little shithead, you've burnt me legs. You ungrateful little bugger. Come here!"

While he's swearing and moaning, I take advantage, fumbling for the door catch. I find it and pull – it gives and I'm out and running.

The ground's uneven, I stumble on something in the long grass and nearly crash down but I manage to stay upright and pelt forwards, running blindly. I can't see where I'm heading. I've just got to get away. Behind me I hear the car start up, hear the engine rev, hear the spin of wheels in the mud. He's got to turn the car round, I might have a chance. I might find somewhere to hide.

The ground slopes uphill. Gasping for breath, I clamber up through thistles and brambles making for a high fence, hoping there's a gap I can slip through. But when I reach the top I see the fence is made of smooth sheets of overlapping metal – there's no chance. Light blares over the top of the wall and outlined against the purple sky I see factory roofs. I'm not in the bloody countryside like I thought but on some industrial wasteground with a high fence enclosing it. I'm trapped. The pervy driver's car is below me, positioned sideways across a track. He'll be able to see me up here.

My eyes sweep across the scrubby land. The car drove in here so there has to be a way out. I run along the fence and then I spot it, a dark gap. The car engine roars as I head towards freedom. I hear wheels swerving and spinning, churning up mud. I zigzag down the hill and on to the track. The gap's only a few metres away, headlamps scorch my heels. He's driving fast, revving hard, I've had it.

The car's alongside me, I try to run faster, my chest bursting, my throat on fire. The car window's down, I can see him, then, *slam*, I'm knocked sideways, sent sprawling. My arm jars, pain racing through it, sharp thorns scratch at my face. I cough, squirm on to my knees and wipe dirt from my mouth.

When my eyes are focusing again, I see my bag half-buried in the grass beside me, that must be what knocked me off my feet, he's thrown it at me. I double over, feeling sick and winded but at the same time, relieved. I've got my stuff and he's cleared off, disappeared through the gap, his tail lights dissolving into the night.

I rest my head on the bag, my stomach rolling and heaving. I try to calm myself by taking big deep breaths;

sick wells in the back of my throat. I retch and spew on to the grass. When I try to stand up my legs feel weak but I get myself together, pick up my bag and totter towards the gap in the fence then out into the road.

Opposite me, there's a big sweep of factory gates and a wide drive. I pick up my pace, hurrying past. I begin to feel stronger as I walk down a dark lane, then I turn a corner and find myself in an avenue with trees on one side and terraced houses on the other, the trees are all about the same height and spaced at regular intervals.

I walk as if I'm in a dream. There's the tall glass front of the sports centre, the playground with swings and slides. I know this place! It leads to the park entrance. The sodding twister. He had no intention of taking me to Derby, he just drove round Chesterfield, up and down amongst the houses waiting for me to drop to sleep. I'm almost back where I started, where he picked me up, I haven't gone anywhere!

I throw my bag down in disgust, kick it and then slam it into the railings. I'd like to tear up one of those long spikes, shove it through his car windscreen and stab it into his head. He's long gone, though. Gone to pick up some other kid. Pervy bastard, sick psycho. If I get a chance I'll tell the scuds about him – they should lock him up.

I push at the big iron gates but they don't open. I rattle them so violently I'm surprised nobody comes running, then I try pushing and lifting them but they don't give and I end up spluttering with rage. I've failed. I should be in Derby, settled in Gran's house waiting to get Him but I've ended up just a few minutes' walk away from Jill's house. Everything I do is crap, that day when I was in the garden and I saw Him coming round the corner in his manky car, I should have run away. Mum would have been better off without me – she might still be alive.

I wipe my face on my pot arm, slide down the railings and sit on the gravel. It's cold, my fingers are freezing and my ears are like ice-cream cones. I don't know what to do. I can't go back to Jill and Eric, they're probably out looking for me, furious I've done a bunk and angry cos they'll have to explain my disappearance to Miss SW.

I lean on my good elbow and pull my anorak hood tightly round my neck. No, I can't go back home but I don't fancy spending the night here, either. I've got to try and get inside the park, at least in there I'll find some shelter, I'll climb over if I have to. I get to my feet and check the gate again. It's definitely locked but then I notice a side gate and when I push that, it clangs open.

I trudge through into a silent world, the grass is wet fur, bushes hover like ghosts. A cold wind blasts across the open space freezing my skin. By the lake the path is shadowy and uneven, my feet crunch on the gravel. I'm not sure in which direction to go but when I see the bulky shape of the cricket pavilion looming, I head towards it. A single light is shining above its veranda and I begin to feel warmer as I hurry towards it. Taking a short cut I skip over a low stone wall and cut through a flower bed. As I get closer I hear voices. A few more steps and I make out the shapes of bicycles, huddled figures and the glowing lights of cigarettes. Somebody shouts,"Hey, who goes there?" I dodge back through the flower bed, hide behind a hedge, my heart pounding. When I've made sure that nobody's coming to look for me I hurry in the opposite direction.

My shoes squelch on the wet grass. My good arm is aching from carrying the heavy bag and as I skirt round the edge of the football pitch I'm blasted by icy gusts of wind. I don't know where to go. I just keep walking until I come to a bank. I climb up the slope and stop – below me is the black strip of the river, one solitary light sparkling on its inky surface. I step forward and the ground falls away.

I begin to slide, down and down. My bag is almost torn from my grasp, the backs of my legs scrape against rock, I roll sideways and my head thumps against something hard. I try to wedge my feet into the bank but I can't. I fall and bounce until my bag slams on to a hard, flat surface and I'm jolted to a stop. I slump, panting and wheezing, my back against the slope. I've found a place to hide all right, I'm at the stinking river's edge in the middle of some bushes.

When I've got my breath back I gently touch my head

and feel a sore wet patch – I've cut myself. I start to panic. What if it's bad? What if it's like Mum's wound? Then I'll keel over and bleed to death and nobody will know where I am. They'll find me cold and stiff, dead as a frozen chicken. I don't really care about dying but I've got to get Him first.

I squeeze my eyes tight to stop myself crying, stamp my feet on the ground and then turn round to look for a way back up the bank. Above me I hear voices, somebody shouts, then a stone plops into the water. I flatten myself against the rough grass. There's more shouting and crazy giggling, show-off laughter – it sounds like a bunch of lads.

Somebody yells. "Go on, Rob, chuck it in."

"You do it, yer puny chicken."

A boulder comes rolling down the bank. I dodge sideways and it just misses my shoulder. I wonder if they've seen me, if they're doing it on purpose.

"Hey, Tyson, lob that one in as well."

I stand rigid with fear wondering if something heavy's going to crash on my head. There's a shriek and a missile comes flying past, landing in the water with a big splash. The lads cackle in triumph. I hope they'll go now they've had their fun but suddenly one of them shouts, "Hey up, somebody's down there."

"Where?"

"Nah, it's a log, you divvy."

"It's somebody, I'm tellin' ya."

"Chuck something at it then, see if it moves."

I tremble and cower into the curve of the bank hoping that anything they throw at me will miss. A handful of pebbles rolls down. I wish I had Griffy with me, I could pretend she was fierce.

"It's somebody. Look, you can see a face."

"Hey you, are yer goin' to jump in?" More laughs.

"We'll 'elp you if you like."

They're wettin' themselves now, thinking they're hilarious. A stone zings past my head. I drop my bag and cover my face with my good hand.

"Hey, homeless. Come up, we won't hurt yer."

"Could be somebody escaped from prison, could be a murderer."

"Yeah."

I hear a heavy stone thundering down. I start to run along the river bank, I can't see where I'm going, my feet slip on mud, a clump of trees blocks my way. The lads shout and one of them starts to scramble down the bank.

Then there's a sharp cry. "Bloody hell. Me hand, I've cut me bloody hand."

He's stopped halfway down the bank, shouting and yelling. "Come over 'ere, yer stupid twats. I need help. Me hand's busted. It's bleedin' buckets. Get me up!"

Clods and stones roll down as he scrambles higher. His mates reach down to pull him up, they're crackin' up, giggling fit to bust.

"It's not funny. I'm bleedin' to death."

They drag him up and hurry off, their shouts floating into the night air. I wait, my body pressed into the spiky twigs and brambles. When I'm sure they've gone, I look up. The sky's a dark billowy grey, a lone star is shining. I drop to the floor and sob, torrents of tears soaking my face.

I don't know how long I lie there crying, I'm past caring. Part of me feels like rolling over and falling into the river and ending it all. The world's shite and I'd be better off dead. I'm not sure about heaven and stuff like that but it might be true, I might be happy – me and Mum dancing to Radio One and eating ice-cream Mars bars.

It's the cold seeping into my shoes that jolts me to my senses. I'm lying with my feet in a muddy patch and water's icing my toes. I sit up, thinking I'll rub some warmth back into them, but both trainers are caked in mud. I stand up and start wandering about, looking for where I dropped my bag, my legs are unsteady and I wobble like I'm drunk. Eventually I stumble into the bag and I start the grim climb up the slope – two steps up, one sliding back. Halfway up I stop to rest, sitting on a ledge. I'm panting hard and the fingers of my good hand are burning from grasping at twigs and bushes. I swallow hard, drop my chin on to my chest and rock gently backwards and forwards. All I want to do is go home.

eight

Jill opens the door, her eyes widen to saucers when she sees me. "Oh, David. Thank goodness. We've been so. . ."

She doesn't finish what she was going to say but rushes out and throws her arms round me. Then she pulls me inside. "Thank goodness you're back."

She holds me at arm's length and looks at me. "What happened? You've hurt your head. Oh my God, David. Come inside quickly, let's get you sorted." She shouts over her shoulder. "Eric, it's all right. He's back."

Eric meets us in the hall. "Crikey, David. Where on earth have you been? What a state!"

"He needs a hot bath," Jill says. "He's frozen."

She's about to steer me upstairs when Griffy comes tearing in and throws herself at me. I bend to hug her warm body.

When I straighten up, Jill's shaking her head at Eric.

She squeezes my shoulder. "Come on, let's go into the kitchen and look at that cut. Eric, will you go and run the bath?"

"Righto," Eric says and retreats upstairs.

Jill steers me into the kitchen and sits me down next to the radiator. I bend thankfully towards the heat, my cheeks stinging. Jill places a thick coat round my shoulders smoothing it over my pot arm, she fusses round me clucking sympathetically. I give myself up to it, glad to feel safe and warm.

I hear her fiddling about with the kettle and she puts a bowl of warm water on the table.

"Don't worry, I'll be gentle."

She starts dabbing at my head with cotton wool, the water trickles down my forehead and blooms red in the bowl.

"This will sting a bit," she says, as she shakes some drops from a bottle on to a fresh piece of cotton wool. I wince as the antiseptic seeps into the cut. Jill stands back and pats my shoulder. "That's better," she says. "It's not as bad as I thought, just a nasty scratch, thank goodness. Now, what about some hot chocolate?"

I'm vaguely aware of her rattling around in cupboards and clanging saucepans. Any minute I expect her to turn and yell at me but she doesn't and I'm thankful because I'm having enough trouble. Violent shivering has overtaken me and I'm shuddering like a crazy ghost. I feel dizzy but when I close my eyes it's worse. I hear the stupid yobbos shouting, remember the numbing fear of being trapped in the car and, clear as a cartoon, I see the pervy man's smile, his lips wet with saliva and I hear his words – "You wouldn't mind doing me a little favour, would you?" I shudder as I think what might have happened if I hadn't escaped.

Jill puts steaming mugs of chocolate down on the table.

"David, are you all right?"

I open my mouth and all the horror in my head nearly comes tumbling out. I want to tell her about the pervy man and the idiot lads and everything else that is jammed inside my brain but, just in time, I remember why I cleared off, what made me run away. She wasn't going to stop Miss SW handing me over to Him. I can't trust her. She'd have put me in his clutches, and he'd be thrilled, he'd have made sure I kept my mouth shut.

Jill pulls a chair up close to mine. "We were worried sick about you, David. Eric's been all over town looking for you. Why didn't you come back when it was dark?"

I don't see what darkness has to do with anything. What difference does it make whether it's dark or light? I ran away, I ran away because I couldn't trust anybody.

Jill sips her drink and clears her throat. "You've got to talk to us, David. We can't go on like this. I've got to know what's troubling you. You didn't run off for nothing."

I sit and hold on to the radiator, avoiding her eyes.

"Is there something you want to tell me?"

I reach for a mug and burn my mouth as I sip the hot chocolate.

"Where were you, David? Where did you go?"

I can feel her straining with every nerve, ready to hear the words she wants me to say but I'm not talking, they can all go to hell. I sip my drink in silence. She sighs and Eric comes in.

Jill turns away. "He won't tell me anything," she says.

Eric puts his hand on her shoulder. "Just give him time. He's tired."

There's an edge to Jill's voice. "I'm tired," she says.

"I know," he says. "So am I. It's been a difficult day. Tell you what, let David have a bath while I make us something to eat. I bet we'll all feel better then, bet you're hungry, aren't you, David?"

The question hangs in the air as mechanically I get up and go through to the hall. At the bottom of the stairs I hear Eric say quietly, "I've informed them he's back."

Up in the bathroom I strip off my clothes and slide into the warm soapy water. My body tingles all over as the warmth hits me. I lie back and swish the suds around. I'm tired, my head aches and feels heavy. I've got to make another plan, I've got to get Him but I can't think straight, better if I don't think, shut my brain down, lie and soak, watch the bubbles bursting, tiny rainbows of light, *pop*.

Eric shouts up the stairs telling me dinner's on the table. We eat in silence. I've only picked at my food since I came to live here but now I shovel in forkfuls of shepherd's pie like it's the last meal I'll ever eat. I don't know why, it's like the more I eat the less I'll remember, the food'll soak up the bad memories. I see that Jill's not eating much though. She nibbles at some broccoli, then she pushes the rest of the food round her plate. She puts her knife down and raises a hand to her forehead, massaging the skin as if she's wiping away a stain.

"I'm glad you came back, David, but I wish you hadn't gone in the first place. I wish you'd told me what was bothering you. It's so difficult when we can't talk. I can only guess at what you're thinking."

She rubs at her eyebrows. "Aren't you happy here, David?"

Happy, that's a laugh.

Eric covers Jill's hand with his own. "He'll come round," he whispers. "Don't worry, you're doing a great job."

Jill shakes her head and sighs again. "I'm not so sure. I don't know if I'm helping or not."

Her voice trails off into silence. Eric lifts her hand and lightly kisses her fingertips. He looks at me. "I'm sure David won't be so keen to go off again. I think he's learnt his lesson. It doesn't seem to have been a very enjoyable experience. Let's leave it at that for now, shall we?" he says.

Jill nods and gets up to clear the table. Eric takes an apple from the bowl, throws it into the air and catches it.

"What would you like to do this weekend, David?" he asks. "I thought I might do a spot of fishing on Saturday morning. Want to join me? Of course, fishing's not for everyone – too quiet." He pauses, twirling the apple round on his palm. "Some Saturdays I go and watch Chesterfield play, would you like that?"

He watches me, gauging if I'm showing any interest. Did my eyes flash when he said fishing or football? I'm not keen on either. Certainly not football. He went every Saturday, yelling his head off.

Eric waves his fork looking excited. "Hey, I've just remembered. Chesterfield are playing Derby in the Worthington cup next week, should be a good game and there's two tickets going begging. Rob, my boss at work, got tickets but he can't go. How about it, David – would you like that? Are you a Rams supporter?"

My mind whirls, cogs turning. I don't want to go and watch some crappy football match. But if it's Derby, he's a real Derby fan, never used to miss a game. He might risk it, might come to the match, might not be able to resist. And if he's there, I'll spot Him. I'll find Him, talk to Him, make Him think I want to see Him.

I'll have to be crafty, as crafty as Him. I'll arrange to meet him somewhere quiet, and then. . .

My heart thumps with excitement. I feel blood rush to my cheeks. I look at Eric and give a quick nod.

He beams. "Oh, that's great."

Jill looks happier too. "So, no more running away, David?" she asks.

I'm only too happy to nod. And I don't mind being banished to my room when Jill says I need an early night. I can lie in bed and think up a new plan. This is my first piece of good luck. Perhaps I won't have to go and find Him – he just might come to me.

nine

It's the morning of the match. As soon as I wake, my stomach churns. This afternoon I might see Him. He could be in the crowd. Could be watching the game, shouting for Derby. I'll creep up behind him, pretend I'm glad to see him, wait for the right moment and then strike. Stab him straight through the heart. Thrust my knife in quick, hard, deep. He gasps, clutches at his chest. Blood stains his shirt, spills through his fingers.

I close my eyes. Cold shudders run through me like shock waves. Panic whirls through me like icy water. I don't know if I can do it. I haven't even got a knife.

You idiot; you stupid prat-faced pillock. I bang my head down on the pillow, I hit my thigh with a balled-up fist. *How are you ever going to kill him if you're scared shitless just thinking about it? You're useless.* I slam my body sideways and roll out of bed.

In the kitchen Jill and Eric are busy; dishes and pans clattering, bacon frying.

Eric sets a plate of eggs and bacon down on the table. "Come on, tuck in, it'll set you up for the day."

I'm not hungry but just to be sociable I break off a piece of bread and dip it in egg yolk.

"Looking forward to the match?" Eric asks.

I bite off a tiny chunk of bread, and chew.

"Better not shout too loud for the Rams," he says.

Jill stops slicing bread and flashes him a warning.

"All I mean is, we're sitting with the home supporters," he protests.

"Hmm," Jill says.

I don't mind him joking about me not talking. It makes me feel normal. Shame is, I'm not. My life isn't normal. It's like a big hole, a big black hole filled with maggots and worms, maggoty wormy creatures, like those stupid yobs throwing stones at me in the park, and the sweaty pervert in the car – he was a sick slimy worm. And the biggest slug of all – Him. I hate Him. I look at the bread knife lying in the middle of the table. It has a long serated blade, I plan to steal it.

Griffy nudges me; she's waiting patiently under the table.

"This bacon's good," Eric says. "Better than that watery supermarket stuff."

I slide a piece off my plate and slip it to Griffy. She

thinks it's good too. She licks her lips and puts a paw on my leg.

"Have you been to a cup match before, David?"

Jill still asks me questions even though I never answer. She waits, then carries on as if I had.

"Should be exciting. Pretty noisy though. Will you be all right?"

Eric laughs. "Oh, I should think so. David will look after me."

"Very funny," Jill says, her eyebrows shooting up.

Eric smiles and nods at me. "David will be fine. He'll enjoy it. Take his mind off things."

I look down at my plate. Things – that's one way of describing all the stuff eating away at my brain, all the questions oozing through my mind. How do you stab somebody? Does a knife slide easily between the ribs? Do you twist it? Leave it in or pull it out?

I slip another piece of bacon to Griffy, she sucks it in with a loud slurp.

"That dog never used to beg," Jill comments as she starts to clear the table.

I get up and carry my plate to the sink.

"Oh, thanks. If you're going to wash up I'll go and get changed," Jill says. "Be off to town before it gets busy."

"Good lad," Eric says bringing more dishes over to me.

Huh, did they give me a choice? I run hot water and squirt in loads of washing-up liquid. Bubbles billow like candy floss. I dip the cups into the scalding water.

"Leave you to it, then," Eric says. "I'll be in the office."

If there's one job around the house I can do, it's washing up. Mum taught me how to do it properly. Glasses and cups first, before the water gets greasy, then plates and cutlery, and pans last. It's not easy operating with one hand, though, takes me twice as long. When I've finally washed all the stuff on the worktop I go to the table to see if there's anything left. The breadboard's lying there with the bread knife on top. I pick up the knife and run my thumb down its long jagged edge. It leaves a white stripe on my thumb but no blood, it's not sharp enough.

I open the cutlery drawer and see rows of knives, forks and spoons; a pointed potato peeler; a small sharp knife. I pick it up, the blade's not long enough.

My mouth's gone dry, my breathing's quickened, when I open the second drawer my hand is trembling. *Come on, David, get a grip*. There're a few tea towels, a roll of tin foil – and – underneath, an oblong brown box. My fingers fumble with the catch, I open it and there it is, like it's waiting for me, the perfect murder weapon – smooth wooden handle, clean sharp blade. I pull it out. Long enough to do the job, short enough to conceal. I press my thumb to the edge, a jewel of bright blood blooms – it's lethal.

I check the hallway, slip over to the cloakroom and slide the knife into the inside pocket of my anorak. Glancing over my shoulder I check I haven't been seen, then I straighten up and breathe out a long sigh; sparks of excitement surge through me. In a few hours I'll be at the match, if he's there, I'll find Him. I nod and smile. He doesn't have a clue what's coming.

The town is having a party. Flags and streamers flutter from shop fronts and in the newsagent's there's a big WE'RE ON OUR WAY TO WEMBLEY sign. Traffic piles up at the roundabout as we wait to cross. Blue and white pennants fly from car aerials and radios blare out pre-match news.

It gets even busier and noisier as we turn into the street that leads up to the ground, Groups of lads straddle the road, waving scarves and chanting, "CHESTERFIELD, CHESTERFIELD, CHESTERFIELD". The traffic slows and cars hoot as drivers try to get round the gangs. One lad swears and bangs on a car bonnet as it inches past.

All the noise and chaos makes me feel twitchy and I'm as nervous as a trapped rabbit to start with. When Eric puts a hand on my shoulder, I'm thankful for it. He steers me along the inside of the pavement and then we cross in front of the ground's big blue gates.

We're in the queue at the turnstile when I look round and see a massive horse coming up close behind us.

It's dancing sideways and the scud on top is talking to it. "Steady, steady," he says as he pulls on the reins. I step back. If it gallops into us we'll be flattened; its tail is twitching and it's snorting and stamping. I wouldn't be surprised if it took off. I bet it's sick to its back teeth of noisy football supporters.

The horse stands guard while we wait to go in but just before it's our turn to go through the turnstile, a lad in front of us is stopped and searched. My insides fizz and churn as I watch. They don't find anything, he's let through, but when Eric shows our tickets I stand with my pot arm across my chest, underneath it my heart is beating fast.

"Going to win today, are we?" the ticket man asks.

"Hope so," Eric replies.

I'm mightily relieved when the turnstile clicks behind us but now I'm inside the ground there's more stuff to face. I hear chanting and see a group of Derby supporters wearing black and white shirts. I remember Him wearing his kit, white sports shirt stamped with the Derby ram. He'd be grinning all over his face if they won, but if they lost, he'd slam into the house and be in a foul mood all night.

The chanting fans are surrounded by scuds. I stand and stare, unable to walk past. Eric grabs my hand. "All right, David?" he asks.

I bite my lip. *You wet jelly. Get a grip. Today could be the day so you'd better shape up and get tough. Right?*

I shake off Eric's hand and clatter after him up some dark steps. When we come out into the open there's the pitch, bright-green with clear white markings and all around it – a sea of blue and white, row upon row, wave upon wave of Chesterfield scarves and shirts and hats. Then, at one end, behind the goal, there's liquorice allsorts, a square of black and white shirts and scarves – the Rams.

The noise is ear-splitting, it's like being in a tunnel with a train. There's millions of people shouting. How am I ever going to spot Him in all this lot? I was mad to even think about it. I was crazy to come.

"Along here, there's our seats, follow me."

Eric points, then weaves his way along the row, past outstretched legs and stamping feet. I can't follow him, I'll be trapped.

He turns. "Come on, David. Up here."

I stand and stare. A man with wild grey hair grabs my arm. "Tha wants to hurry up, or else some other bugger'll bag tha seat."

He propels me down the row in Eric's direction. I'm passed from one spectator to another. I suppose they think I'm a right idiot.

"There you are, lad," the last man says. "Sit down. You'll be all right next to me."

"Oh aye, Joe'll protect you from all the hooligans," a man in a blue bobble hat says. "One sight of Joe and they change sides."

All the men laugh because Joe is old and thin and doesn't look like he could steal a fairy from a Christmas tree.

Joe waves his fists. "I can still do you anyday," he boasts.

Everybody laughs again, then one man starts chanting, "FOUR NIL, FOUR NIL" and loads of people join in.

Eric passes me a mint. "Ten minutes to kick off," he says.

I sit back in my seat and suck while I scan the rows of figures opposite. Most of them are wearing blue and white but then there's a gap and the liquorice allsorts begin. I see somebody that could be Him – tall, dark-haired. I stare until my eyes blur but I can't be sure; it could be anybody.

The Derby team run on to the pitch to loud boos and then Chesterfield run on and everybody's up on their feet, stamping and clapping.

The man in the blue bobble hat points at me. "What's wrong with 'im? Is he a Derby supporter?"

I blush. Eric bends down and gives me the programme. "Here, David see who's playing."

The names of the Chesterfield squad – the Spireites – are announced over the loud speaker and at each name the crowd cheers. They mean nothing to me.

A woman pushes past with a girl in tow. The girl whines, "Hurry up, Mum. It's startin'."

I hear a whistle. The crowd roars. I try to concentrate but time and time again my eyes are drawn back to the tall, dark figure in the opposite stand. The players run up and down, occasionally the ball comes close. I don't think anybody's winning.

The chanting comes in waves. "Come on Spireites, come on Spireites."

"Oh, look at that," Joe shouts. "Derby'll get one if they're not careful."

But Derby don't score. Play goes back down the other end and suddenly the crowd erupts.

"Goal, goal, goal. Bloody brilliant, goal!"

I didn't see it but the Spireites are clapping and cheering so I know it's Chesterfield that's scored.

"Brilliant, eh? Brilliant goal," Eric asks me, his face flushed with excitement.

"He's not with it, is he?" Joe says.

Eric ignores him. The crowd chants, "Blue Army's goin' to Wembley."

After this goal there's a lull. The excitement dies down. Joe offers me a polo. He says Chesterfield are playing it safe – they want to be leading when they go in at half-time. Eric agrees but a woman behind him yells, "Playin' safe – who do they think they are? Man United? They should be pushin' forward. You can't relax with a one nil lead."

I can't relax because I keep thinking about Him. He could be over there in that block of Derby fans. He might be one of them shouting at the ref or screaming for a penalty. He might look over when they're taking a throw in and see me. I don't want that. I want to surprise him. I don't want him coming looking for me.

I huddle down in my seat, making myself as unobtrusive as possible until half-time. Chesterfield are still in the lead so everybody round me is happy. When the whistle goes people stand up, shout to friends, thump each other on the back and start making plans to go to the final. Some people push past to get refreshments. Eric says he has to go to the toilet.

"Do you want to go?"

I shake my head.

"Stay there, then, it'll be a right crush. Don't move. I'll bring some drinks back."

Joe offers me tea from his flask but I ignore him, I'm scanning the crowd. He tries to talk to me but soon gives up. Instead he gets into an argument with the man in the bobble hat and while he's waving his arms, I slip away.

People are pushing to go down the steps. I'm carried along, my feet hardly touching the ground. I keep a look out for Eric but don't see him anywhere. I squirm under somebody's armpit, grab the rail and totter down the steps. When I see a sign for the toilets I go in the opposite direction.

I scan every face as I pass but it's hard to see far, I'm small and I can't see over people's shoulders.

"You all right, sonny?" a woman asks me.

I ignore her and move away trying to find a bit more space but I just get stuck in the middle of a group of blokes and when I've weaved through them I come up against a barrier. It's a strong metal fence, I can't go no further. I turn round and look back at the sea of blue and white. If I sit on top of the barrier it'll be a good lookout post but then an obvious thought strikes me – *Dur-brain, sometimes you're so thick. You're not likely to spot Him here, are you? This area is for Chesterfield supporters. Somehow you've got to get yourself over to the other side of the ground.*

I stand for a moment working out what to do. Posted along the barrier are stewards who're acting as guards. A man with a big camera goes up to one of them, talks to him and is let through. That's my cue – quick as a flash I'm behind him.

"I'm with him," I say. "Dad!" I shout, as I run after him.

The man turns round and looks puzzled. I zoom past him and rush towards a group of Derby supporters.

When I'm in their midst my courage ebbs. Most of the men sound like Him, same Derby accent, moaning and complaining.

"Useless as a bunch of fairies."

"How much do they pay him?"

"Too bloody much."

Listening to them gives me the shakes. *He could be*

right here, behind you, watching, waiting. A shiver runs through me. *He's got as much reason to get you as you have to get Him.*

I decide to be more careful, keep my head down, look up only occasionally as I move through the crowd. What I need is a safe place, somewhere I can watch from, without being seen. I edge my way towards some food stalls.

A sudden booming voice stops me in my tracks. "Bloody foreigners, what we need is home-grown talent."

I stumble, look up and see a familiar face. My legs almost give way. *It's not Him, it's not Him.* Even so I'm shaken to my bones. It's somebody I've seen before, somebody he knows. I struggle to remember. I hide behind a man in a long mac and watch. The man who shouted takes a can of beer from his pocket, opens it and swigs it down, tipping his head back, then wiping his mouth with the back of his hand. That does it, that action. I know who he is. When me and Mum first left home, we lived with Mum's friend for a while and he used to come Sundays and collect me. We'd go down the pub and he'd play dominoes with his mates. I got bored so I drew their faces on beer mats. The man who's shouting, he was one of them, his name is Tiny.

"Bloody hell, I was ready for that," Tiny says as he drains his can.

"Here have another," a man at the side of him says.

I move out of my hiding place and pretend to be looking for somebody. Tiny opens the new can but just as he's going to drink he turns his head and waves. I can't see who it is he's waving at but I look back at Tiny and now he's mouthing something. I think he's saying "over there" and he's pointing. I still can't see who he's signalling to but the next moment he hands his programme and can of beer to a mate.

"Take care o' them, I'm goin' for a Jimmy Riddle. Back in a mo," he says.

My heart starts thumping fast, he's up to something and whatever it is, I'm going to follow him and find out. Luckily, it's not difficult to keep him in sight – he's taller than most blokes and twice as wide. He heads towards the Gents but then veers off and pushes towards the edge of the crowd.

He's moving purposefully. I'm pretty sure he's meeting somebody and that he wants to keep his meeting secret. I'm just congratulating myself on being Inspector Morse when a gang of lads lurches sideways knocking me off course and I end up sandwiched between two old women.

"What you up to young 'un?" one of them says as she runs her hand over my spiky hair.

"Enjoyin' the game?" the other one asks.

Stupid women, leave me alone. I dodge out of their way and look round but I can't see Tiny anywhere. He should be visible, tall as a lighthouse – but he isn't, he's gone.

I hunch my shoulders and thrust my hands deep in my pockets. Suddenly all the noise comes thundering into my ears, people waving and shouting, others laughing and singing. I want to rush back to the barrier, get back to my seat. Eric will be looking for me, he was going to buy me a drink. I hear a voice coming over the tannoy, they're announcing a lost kid. It isn't me but it will be any minute.

A man turns round and blows a plume of smoke in my face, then he coughs, hacks and spits near my foot. I run to the only place of safety I can see – a space beside the hot dog stand.

I check the queue in front of the stall and then edge round to the side of the stand. There's a pile of cardboard boxes and other stuff round here and some people on crates eating food. I think about sitting down and just waiting till somebody finds me but then I spot Tiny; he's talking to somebody I can't see. I move sideways trying to get a better view and when I see who it is, my heart thumps against my ribs like it's scored a goal. The man is small and skinny with cropped blond hair. He's wearing a black anorak and a Derby scarf. It's been a couple of years since I've seen him but he hasn't changed, it's his best mate – Steve Fawbert.

For a brief second his eyes flick on to mine. He steps forward, I think he's coming over but no, he registers nothing, he doesn't recognize me, he looks away – he hasn't changed but I have.

I blow out a big sigh of relief. My knees are trembling, I know I'm risking it but I've got to stay and watch. And I get lucky. A man comes up and thrusts a burger into my hand.

"Here lad, do you want this? I bought one too many."

I bury my face in the giant-sized cob and look all round in case he's nearby. When I'm sure I can't see Him I focus all my attention on Steve and Tiny. Steve looks nervous, his eyes darting about, but he takes no notice of me, I'm just a little lad feeding his face.

"What's up?" I hear Tiny ask.

Steve keeps his voice low but I can just hear him. "Bloody nerve-rackin' this."

Tiny nods. "Where's 'e now?"

Steve scowls. "He's gone. All that ruddy trouble for forty-five minutes, then 'e buggers off."

I nearly choke on a mouthful of bread. They're talking about Him, they must be.

"What? Where?" Tiny asks.

Steve shrugs his shoulders. "He got scared – all them scuds about, never seen so many."

"He shouldn't 'ave come. They're playin' crap anyway."

"I know but he was going stir crazy, not bin out since it 'appened, didn't even go to the funeral, poor sod."

My heart catapults. I lean closer, desperate to hear more but some kids run past kicking a box and I miss

92

what they say next. I daren't move any closer but I'm desperate for information. Luckily, the next moment the kids come running back and the men move towards me.

I hear perfectly as Tiny asks, "What's the situation now?"

Steve doesn't answer right away, he sighs and shakes his head, then pulls a pack of fags from his pocket. He offers one to Tiny. They both light up before Steve starts talking again.'

"Mart's stumped. 'E wants to tell 'is side but he reckons the scuds'll stitch 'im up. His best hope is Davey – make the lad tell what 'appened but Mart don't know where 'e is."

At this moment Steve looks over at me and catches my eye. I freeze. *Do something you idiot or he'll start to suspect.* With trembling hands I make a big deal of balling up the hamburger wrapper and throwing it in the air. I'm pushing my luck, I should clear off but I can't.

When the kids come running past again, I take the opportunity to slip behind some tall gas cylinders. Peeping from between them I've got a clear view of both men.

Steve draws on his cigarette and coughs. He says something I don't catch but then he turns his head and his voice reaches me. "Mart wants 'elp finding the kid. I'm meeting him after the match, pub called The

Peacock, bottom of the market place, room at the back."

Tiny nods. "All right, I'll be there." He starts to walk away but he's only gone a couple of steps when Steve darts forward and grabs him.

"Don't bring nobody else, right?"

Tiny nods and hurries off. Steve waits a few moments, then he goes. I slump to the floor leaning my back against the cylinders. I'm shaking and my stomach's gone all squelchy. I swallow and then breathe slow and deep, I've got to be strong. This is my chance. I've got to seize it, get to the slimy bastard before he gets me. They've told me where to find Him – usual place – with his mates inside a pub. Today might be different though, today might be a big surprise. I put my hand inside my anorak pocket and touch the cold steel blade.

ten

As the second half kicks off, I'm pushing through the turnstile and out towards town. Eric will go spare when he realizes I've gone but I can't waste time worrying. I've got bigger things to think of and if I complete my mission I'll never be allowed to live with him and Jill anyway. I'll be locked up, shut away like a lunatic and I won't care. As long as he's dead, as long as I've wiped Him off the face of the earth, I don't give a toss.

Alert for trouble, I walk along the main road and cross at the traffic lights. My eyes and ears act like radar, bouncing off cars and passers-by. This busy road is bad news, so, at a crossroads, I turn off and dodge down a side street.

Wrong move. Outside a cafe, two scuds are leaning against a patrol car. They've seen me so I can't leg it. I saunter past. The car radio bursts into life. Crackle, buzz, a voice from outer space. I imagine the message.

Missing. Thirteen year old boy, small for his age, short, spiky hair, broken arm, acts dumb. I imagine footsteps pounding after me, imagine a hand on my shoulder. But nothing happens. I reach the end of the street safely and when I stop and glance behind me, the scuds haven't moved.

There's something going off though. Another patrol car's pulled up, the door's opening, a woman with short skirt and blonde ponytail is getting out. Gardner! I gulp in a gobful of air and belt like a mad dog, as far away from them as I can.

My heart's exploding, my chest's on fire as I stagger on to some wasteground. Frantic for a place to hide I spin round looking in all directions. Over at the far end I spot a big rubbish skip, head over and collapse behind it.

Gasping for breath I look to see if I've been followed. Nothing, nobody – just the cold wind stirring the gravel, flattening the weeds; I've avoided capture. Now, with a bit of luck, I can find and stake out the pub.

I slip a hand into my pocket and touch the blade of my knife. When I hear a car roaring towards me, my fingers stiffen and close round the handle. Wheels shudder on the gravel, swish through long grass. Fear fills my mouth. The scuds have come for me. I wait with every nerve dancing. Do I run or stay put? Slowly, carefully, I peer round the side of the skip.

Phew! Relief! It's not a patrol car but a beat-up truck dripping with rust. The engine's still running, the doors open and two men get out and wander over to where there's a pile of twisted metal and car tyres. One of them bends down and examines the tyres. He picks one up and rolls it to his mate who slings it in the back of the truck.

I wait till they've climbed in and driven off, check again to make sure no scuds are around, then I'm away, racing over the gravel and into a car park, weaving through rows of cars, running down steps and smack into a busy street. Cross the road, up a narrow cobbled alley and out into the big market square.

Colour and noise flare in my face like fireworks. Rows of stalls blaze with fruit and woolly jumpers; stallholders call out their bargains and people meet and babble. It's as busy as the football match. I'd like to run home. I wish I was curled up on the sofa with Griffy snuggled beside me. But I know the match will be finished soon – I have to be ready.

Desperately, I scan the square. I can't see far; too much stuff in the way. I dodge through some stalls and come out at the bottom end, opposite some shops. That's better. My eyes sweep to left and right, clocking everything. Shock shudders through me – coming towards me is a huge, brown horse. It's from the football match, they've sent the mounted police after me! Then I see the blinkers, the feathery feet, the cart. *Idiot*.

It stands so close I can smell it, watch it breathe, its whole side heaving in and out. I'm stuck; have to wait while a man shovels rubbish into its cart, then, when it moves off, I carry on with my quest.

Marks and Spencer's, Boots, McDonalds, shoe shops, travel places, but no Peacock. Shit! What if I didn't hear right? What if Steve said some other place? I scurry round the square, darting round shoppers and squinting down alleyways. I find two pubs – Royal Oak and White Lion, but not the pub I want. I'll have to ask somebody. I stand and watch people hurrying past. I choose a woman with a kind face.

"The Peacock?"

"Yes."

She shakes her head. "I'm new here. Don't know any peacocks, duck."

The next person I ask doesn't even stop. Perhaps they don't hear me. I'm out of practice at speaking.

Two young girls wander by. I follow them and when I'm level, I ask my question. They stare at me like I'm an alien, then collapse into fits of giggles and run off.

I kick the cobblestones. This is stupid, I'm wasting time. I should be at the pub now, hiding, waiting. I sit for a while on the bottom of a stone fountain, then wander about watching the stallholders pack away, it's going dark, the match must be over.

Behind me the clip-clop of hooves echoes sharply. I turn and see the big horse steaming towards me. I move out of its way then watch as it ploughs past and along the bottom of the square. The cart sways behind, moving along the parade of shops, then it disappears. It's vanished. And suddenly I'm running. I curse myself under my breath. *Idiot! Dumbo! Bug brain, no brain.* There are two market squares in Chesterfield, a big one and a little one; the horse is off to collect rubbish from the little square.

I dodge round a van, crash past piles of boxes, zoom along the pavement and as the street lights come on I keep running till I'm through to the smaller square.

The horse is standing stone-still in front of the toilets. I flash past it then stop and stare, my heart pumping, my eyes sweeping backwards and forwards. And I see it, lit by a string of fairy lights – a black and white building with a swinging sign – The Peacock.

In the pub doorway I struggle to catch my breath. My heart's thumping so hard my ribs hurt and my stomach's crawling with nervous spasms. Is he inside already? He's crafty, I know that. When Mum and me were on the run he always found us, sussed out all our tricks, so I know he's smart. He'll make sure the scuds don't catch him.

I hunch my shoulders and huddle into the corner of the porch trying to make myself invisible. What will I do if I see Him? A plan, I've got to have a plan. But all I can think of is, attack, attack! Jump Him, stab Him, kill Him. Bang, quick, hard, fast. Don't flinch, don't back away. *Find the courage – do it!*

The pub door opens and two men practically fall out into the street. A heavy sickly smell pinches my nostrils – cigarette smoke and beer. It reminds me of Him. My mouth goes dry, my breathing quickens, I feel he's near. A room at the back. That's what they said.

I creep round the side of the pub and down an alleyway. It's more like a tunnel with a high brick wall. Then it opens out into a courtyard with a few wooden tubs and tables.

There's nobody about so I dart across to where there's a stack of silver barrels and behind them, a small window. I squeeze through the barrels and crouch under the glass. Slowly, carefully, bit by bit, I straighten up and peer through.

The window looks into a back room. It's large and dimly lit with a long bar at one end. At first it seems empty but when I press my cheek against the glass and stare into a corner, I see the dark shadow of a man.

I stare at the shadow, my eyes bulging, desperate to know if it's Him. I'm concentrating so hard that when there's a noise behind me, I jump and bang my pot arm on a barrel. Damn, it hurts. I grit my teeth and glare at the ginger cat that's knocked over a bottle. But the next moment I realize the cat's done me a favour; footsteps echo down the alley, somebody's coming.

I throw myself at the heavy back door, hoping like hell it'll open. Thankfully, it gives and I stagger through into a dark corridor. Ahead of me is a door and I just make out a sign, GENTS. I dash inside and into a cubicle.

As soon as I'm locked in, the outer door bangs open. Voices echo off the cold bare walls.

"Bloody disgraceful. Slaughtered by a second-division, team."

"Rams my arse. They're nothin' but a bunch of friggin' fairies."

I shrink back against the partition. My heart hammers inside my chest. The voices sound familiar – I'm pretty sure it's Steve and Tiny.

"Three nil," one of them moans.

"Talk about Rams. More like Lambs – lambs to the bloody slaughter."

I hardly dare breathe and when I do, the thick smell of disinfectant gets up my nose, tickling and prickling, making me want to sneeze. I struggle to hold it in and end up making a loud snorting noise. Luckily, at that very moment, the urinal flushes, gurgling and swishing. When it stops, silence descends. The men have gone.

As quietly as possible I edge back the bolt, peer out and when I see it's clear, I zip out fast, back into the corridor. For a moment I stand staring at the door which must lead to the back room. Was it Him, waiting in the corner? If I go through, will he be there? I could be on him before he sees me, stab him before he has time to react. He'd be gobsmacked. Wouldn't know what had hit him. Slam into his heart – thump on the floor. The thought of it nearly makes me laugh out loud.

I'm thinking so hard that I don't even flinch when the door bangs open behind me. And I still haven't moved when a crowd of Chesterfield supporters surges past and carries me along on a giant wave. They're laughing and singing and one of them snatches me up and lifts me on to his shoulder.

"Come on, sonny. Let's celebrate. Up the Spireites, eh?"

The crowd propels me forward and through into the back room where I'm plonked down on a stool at the bar.

"You're Jim's lad, aren't you?" the man who carried me in asks.

I'm too shocked to answer, suddenly everything's spun out of control. Luckily the man doesn't seem to mind, he's too busy waving his pals over to the bar.

"Come on, come and have a drink."

I want to turn and look into the corner, see if he's here. If he is, has he seen me? I've got to look, I need to know, but just as I'm about to swivel round, a small, fat man bangs into my stool.

"Sorry, duck," he says.

"This is Jim's lad," the man tells him.

"Oh aye," the fat man says. "Jim'll be in any minute."

I've no idea who Jim is but it might be a problem if he arrives. For now though, I'm all right. The men are shielding me from view while they prattle on.

"I can't believe it," one of them says. "If you'd told me yesterday that Chesterfield would beat Derby by three goals, I'd have said you were jokin'."

I try to look excited, smiling when they look at me but I'm waiting for my chance to slip away.

A younger man comes up, thumps one of the men on the shoulder and laughs. "Well, the best team won, eh? That's all that matters, eh?" He leans over the bar. "Oi, barman. Let's have some service down here. Come on, drinks all round, eh?"

"Who's payin'?" the barman asks.

"You are," he says.

As everybody laughs I slip off my stool. There's a crush of bodies at the bar now and I try to weave my way through them. I dodge behind a group of teenagers and pretend to tie my laces. When the crowd shifts, I get a clear view of the corner.

They're there. Steve and Tiny sitting facing me and opposite them is a man with broad shoulders and long dark hair. It's Him. My breathing quickens, I nearly choke as sick rises in the back of my throat. He's sitting drinking beer; he leans forward to catch something Tiny says then he sits back, his shoulders shaking. He's laughing – he's sitting in a pub laughing and Mum's dead.

I lean against a table, my hand touches the outside of my pocket, I feel the shape of the knife. *Come on, go to him. Pretend you're missing him, act upset, take him somewhere quiet. Then, slam, you've got Him.*

I'm edging my way through to the corner when somebody shouts, "Hey, what're you Derby lot doin' in 'ere?"

Another voice joins in, "You lot haven't got nothin' to celebrate."

Steve starts to get up but Tiny grabs his arm forcing him down. The room's gone suddenly quiet, everyone watching.

All I'm watching is Him. Around him people start to argue and shout but he doesn't move.

One lad in a blue baseball cap seems drunk already, he's swearing at Tiny and Steve. His mate comes up and pushes him into the table and at the same moment a general cry goes up. "Derby supporters."

A group of lads in blue shirts surround the table. Tiny puts his arms out trying to calm things, Steve stands up, but as far as I can see he doesn't move. He sits absolutely still saying nothing.

I'm just wondering how I can get to him when he turns round and looks straight at me. I see his mouth open in surprise. He starts to get up. His hand is on his chair, in another moment he'll grab me. I can't move. My feet are bolted to the floor. But before he steps round his chair somebody reels into him, there's a crash of glass as a drink goes flying and all hell breaks loose. Seats and tables are knocked flying. Tiny lurches towards me, his shirt front soaked with beer. Two men grab him and then it's just a pile of fists and bodies. I'm shoved aside as customers elbow their way out. I get my brain in gear, duck down and head for safety, cowering under the bar.

The barman's ringing a bell and shouting, "Outside, outside. No fighting in here. I'm calling the police."

The crowd sways, bends and huddles like a rugby scrum. I can't see what's happening. There's more shouting and then Tiny pops up, his hand on Steve's shoulder propelling him towards the door. Fists and elbows erupt everywhere, sweaty shoulders clash in their efforts to get to the exit. Giant feet stamp near my fingers, a knee catches mine knocking me backwards. I scramble to my feet, crane my neck, scanning the room – he's gone.

I make my way to the door. Some blokes are standing in the yard. I push past them, run up the dark alley and into the lamplit square. It's quiet now, the traders have packed up and he is nowhere to be seen.

I lean back against the wall and bang my head on the brickwork. Just for good measure I bang it again. I deserve to be punished. He was there and I let him escape. My head's throbbing but I throw myself back, smack at the wall. I was too slow, too bloody slow. I scrape my knuckles on the brickwork, slam my heel into the wall so I'm stabbed with pain. I want to cry. I saw Him, he was there. And I failed.

105

It's quite dark now, the lamps casting big shadows over the pavement. I think about Mum and how she used to draw the curtains as soon as it got dark. It made her feel safer. Tears fill my eyes. Mum's dead, she's never coming back. Mum's dead and he was in the pub, laughing.

I blink back my tears and look across the empty market stalls. I don't know what to do now he's seen me, he could be watching, waiting to get me. He wants me to tell the scuds what happened to Mum. He thinks I'll help clear his name, stupid bastard.

I shrink back into the shadows and pull my coat tight. Across the road by one of the empty market stalls I see two shadows. One is tall and wide and one is much smaller. I think it's Tiny and Steve. I see them light up. Steve stamps his feet and blows out a long plume of smoke. The other, bigger man zips up his coat, puts his hands in his pockets and jiggles his shoulders, his cloudy breath mixes with the cigarette smoke until there's a halo round the pair of them.

I wonder if they're waiting for Him. What other reason could they have to hang about? They'll be taking him back to Derby or to his hiding place.

I decide to stay put and watch them, when right behind me, the front door of the pub crashes open. I jump out of my skin and turn just in time to see some Spireite fans lurch out. They sprawl across the pavement, shouting and chanting. I recognize the lad in the baseball cap as he and his mates head off across the square.

Then I hear him shout. "There they are. Let's get the bastards."

The gang run straight for Steve and Tiny. I hear a crash and some yells and groans. Some people come out of the pub and run off towards the fight. I go with them and arrive to see Tiny on the floor, his face a bloody mess. When he tries to get up the lads show no mercy, they move in, stamping and kicking. I look around hoping Steve will come to his rescue but I can't see him.

Tiny's making a horrible wheezing sound as if all the air's being pressed out of him. I can't stand it. I feel sick, my stomach's heaving. I stumble to the gutter and retch and spit into a drain.

I clutch my coat, trying to stop myself shaking, my throat burns and my mouth is bitter with the taste of vomit. Slowly I stumble towards one of the empty market stalls, circling round, away from the scene of the fight. When I reach the stall I climb on to the empty counter and sit back in its shadow.

I don't know how long it is before the scream of a siren splits the air and an ambulance rumbles over the cobbles. Doors open, a trolley clangs, voices shout. I watch it all from my hiding place. The blue light flashes round the square. Figures move and freeze, crouch and stand. The ambulance doors close. The siren blares through my head.

I sit up and press my fists over my ears, glaring at the crowd of gossipers and gawpers. They stand and watch as the ambulance drives away, the siren blaring into the night.

One spectator stands a little way apart from the crowd. I blink and he shifts slightly, moving into the glow of the pub's fairy lights. He's tall and thin and although I can't see it clearly, I know his face – the long straight nose, the amber eyes – the stare that goes right through you.

Icy fingers grip my throat. I can't move, I can barely breathe. Cold is taking me over, freezing me to a block of ice. If he walks right by me, I won't be able to do a thing; my hands are stiff, frozen popsicles. I do nothing but stare – stare and stare through glistening tears. Then the figure moves and melts away into the shadows. The spell is broken. I lie back on the top of the empty stall, crying with frustration.

You coward. You feeble, weak, pathetic coward. Call yourself a killer? You haven't got the guts.

I curl up into a ball making myself as small as possible. I hate myself. I'm useless. I had my chance and I didn't take it. I'm too soft and weak. I should have killed Him.

eleven

I awake with a jolt. Searing light burns my eyes. I turn my head but the glare's still there, scorching my eyelids. I can't remember where I am. I try to sit up but I'm stiff as cardboard, cold to the bone.

"Stay there, son."

A man's voice. I wriggle and squirm, trying to see who it is behind the dazzling beam. Hands clamp my shoulders, something heavy is thrown around my body. I want to scream but my voice gurgles and turns to mist.

"Are you David?"

Another voice. Two of them. I try to wrench myself backwards but they're holding me down.

"Come on, son. You'll be all right with us."

Faces fracture the light, eyes glitter like glass.

"Are you David Dawson?" one of them asks.

My throat closes up, I can hardly breathe. Who are they? I twist my head, butting at his arm.

"Hey, there's no need for that. We're here to help."

Liar! He's sent them, sent them to kidnap me.

I push against the man's hip, struggling and bucking but I can't break free. They've wrapped me in something tight.

"Easy, easy."

I sink back and close my eyes. Way in the distance I hear one of them say, "Must be him. Can't be many lads sleeping out on a night like this, not with a broken arm, not in Chesterfield."

All the fight in me dissolves. It's no use, they've got me. I'm picked up and slung over a shoulder, folded in two inside the blanket. It's hard to breathe, my head lolls from side to side. I make one last attempt to get free, kicking out wildly but my legs jangle in mid air, useless as a puppets.

"Steady, son. Calm down. We'll look after you."

Piss off. Leave me alone.

"Don't worry, son. Nearly there."

I see the white blur of a car. The door opens. I'm pushed in head first. The seat's hard, a sharp smell of disinfectant stings my nostrils. Slam, the door bangs.

One of the men gets in beside me. He levers me up to a sitting position and props me in the corner. "Bit warmer now, eh, son?"

I'm trembling. I feel so cold my bones ache. And I'm angry, angry I didn't see them coming, angry I'm in their power.

110

From the front a radio blares. "Alpha four, alpha four." The driver answers. "Alpha Four receiving. We've got him. Answers to the description but won't give his name. No visible damage – just cold."

There's a crackle and sizzle and something I can't hear properly, something about hospital. I look at the man in the front. Why is he talking about taking me to hospital, what's going on? I turn and glance at the man sitting beside me. He's wearing a navy blue sweater with a badge on the shoulder. The man in the front is dressed the same way. There's a badge on the steering wheel. Am I stupid or what? *Idiot brain – moron. You were so scared you didn't even notice. You're in a scud car. He didn't send them, the scuds have got you.*

A wave of relief washes through me. I'm thankful the men aren't his mates, at least with the scuds I'm safe, but how long before they start drilling me for information? And I don't want to go to hospital, they can stick that, I'm not going back there. I struggle to free my arm from the tight blanket, feel for the door handle, find it and pull. No escape this time, it's locked.

I stare out of the car window. Images form on the dark glass – the lad in the baseball cap glaring with anger, Tiny's face splattered with blood. Then I see Him, eyes blazing, staring right at me. He saw me in the pub, he was here in the market square, watching, I know it was him. Pictures come flying at me through the dark; twisted faces, clenched jaws, punching fists.

The sound of Tiny's groan and the ambulance blaring into the square echoes through my head. I bang my head back against the seat but I still see the glow of his eyes shining like headlamps, he's haunting me. I shudder and bite the blanket to stop myself from shouting out.

"You all right, son?"

The scud stares at me. He thinks I'm mad. Perhaps I am. Mad, angry, insane, bonkers. I stare back at him. He looks away.

The cop in the front is talking to somebody on the radio. When he's finished he starts up the engine.

"Orders are . . . take him straight home. Doctor's coming out to see him."

His partner laughs. "My God, what's he done to deserve that? Must be royalty." Then he leans across me, his face close to mine, his breath sour. For a crazy moment I think he's going to hit me. I throw my head back, wait for the blow. "Better clip you in," he says.

He reaches for the seat belt, threads it across my chest and bends, struggling to clip it into the catch. His hands fumble. I cringe, I don't want him to touch me.

His sharp cry startles me. "What's this? Feels like you got an iron bar in your coat. What is it, son?"

His hand slides into my pocket, his head rears up sharply. "Bloody hell!" He holds up the knife. "Nearly cut me finger off."

I curl back in the corner, as far away from him as I can.

"I'd better take charge of this," he says. "You might do somebody an injury."

The heater's blasting out now and as the warmth seeps in my skin tingles and itches like it's got nettle rash.

"Straight home. Those was the orders," the driver says.

The car jolts forward and judders slowly over the cobbles. No siren, no flashing light, no zooming off at high speed.

A hand pats my shoulder. "Bet you're glad we found you, eh, son? Frozen as a sausage, you were. You'd have been solid by morning."

I ignore him, staring straight ahead. He's not put off but chunters on. "Not far to your place. Not far at all."

I wish he'd shut up but he doesn't.

"You were at the match today, eh? They won, eh? My God, there's been some celebrating. And some fights, I can tell you."

He talks non-stop, loud as a boxing referee, jabbering away until suddenly, he remembers he's holding the knife. He stares at it a moment then pulls a plastic bag from the seat pocket and wraps it round the knife. "Deal with this later," he mutters.

As we turn up the avenue most houses are in darkness, but number eight blazes with light. I'm unrolled from the blanket, helped out of the car and set on my feet.

"All right, son?"

In answer I totter towards the gate. I stumble, and one of the scuds holds me up – the other goes ahead and knocks loudly on the front door. When it opens, I hear Eric's voice.

My stomach knots up. Now I'm for it. He'll go bananas. I stand still, biting my lip. Eric comes down the path, his face set like concrete. I put my head down, wait for the blow. I feel his eyes on me, boring a hole in my head. I tremble.

"Well you took your time getting home."

His tone is hard and bitter. I chew on my lip and look away.

"So you should be ashamed," he says.

Now, I think. Now, he'll sock me one. He moves closer, in for the kill. I don't flinch. I deserve what's coming. His hand touches my head. But he doesn't hit me. I look up and he's standing shaking his head and when he speaks, his voice is soft. "You missed a good match."

Tears prick my eyes as I follow him. He should have hit me. Knocked me to kingdom come.

I trip on the blanket as I go up the front step and Jill's there to catch me. "Careful," she says, steadying me. Her hair's all wild as if she's been out in the wind and her eyes are watery. "You can't make a habit of

114

this, David," she says sharply. "We're responsible for you, we have to know where you are." She leads me towards the sitting room. "Come on, I've lit the fire."

Nobody's yelling at me. Nobody threatens me. I can't believe it. I'm sitting on the settee in front of the fire and somebody's passing drinks round like it's a party. My eyes flick round from one person to another – Jill and Eric, the two scuds, and over in the corner, Miss Social Worker. What's she doing here in her shimmery dress, looks like she's been out clubbin'. By the pissed off look on her face I reckon she was interrupted mid-snog. I don't care, she shouldn't have bothered interrupting her social life for me.

When her mouth slides into a smile, my insides clench tight as a fist. Her smile's plastic as false teeth, the smile of Dracula. I glare at her.

Sergeant Gardner brings in a tray of tea. "Hi, David," she says, putting the tray down and holding out a steaming mug. "Lucky these two officers found you. It's a cold night."

I look away, ignoring her outstretched hand. I'm not taken in by her soft words, she and Miss SW are in it together. Jill takes the mug and holds it for me.

"Everybody's been really great," Jill says. "We've all been worried about you. Sarah left a party to be here."

Sarah, who's Sarah? I blink and see Miss Social Worker nodding. I want to tell her we don't want her, to go back to her party. In fact, I wish they'd all disappear and leave me alone. I glare at everybody in turn, give them the dead-eye to shut them up and it works for a few minutes. They're quiet and in the silence I hear Griffy barking and scratching.

Eric sighs. "Better let that dog in."

I shiver and sniff. The fire's hot on my face. My skin tightens, tingles, throbs, as if my flesh is melting layer by layer, it's like being tortured, sweat prickles down my back. I wriggle out of my anorak and push it aside, then the door opens and Griffy comes bounding in. She doesn't care what I've done, she's just pleased to see me – ecstatic. She leaps on to my knee, sniffing and snuffling then nuzzling close and flopping down. I bury my face in her fur.

Eric's followed Griffy in and I sense him watching us. "It's no good trying to protect him, Griffy," he says. "He's got a lot of explaining to do."

"I should say so," says one of the scuds. "Carrying a lethal weapon is a serious offence."

All eyes in the room swivel towards me and they're all asking the same question.

Luckily, at that moment the doorbell rings. Jill gets to her feet. "That'll be Kate," she says.

I've no idea who Kate is but I'm glad of her interruption. There are lots of unsaid things in the air as Jill goes into the hall and opens the front door.

"Thanks for coming, Kate," we hear her say and the next moment she's ushering somebody into the room.

"This is David," Jill says.

A girl in a grey coat comes and stands in front of me. She has dark curly hair and big brown eyes. "I've heard a lot about you," she says. She's holding a bag which she drops on the carpet before sitting down beside me. Her dark eyes sweep over me, examining, assessing. "I'm a doctor," she says.

I don't care who the friggin' hell she is. And I don't need a doctor. I'm just cold and tired and I want to go to bed. I lean back so half my face is hidden by the sofa cushion and I close my eyes.

"No use hiding from me," Kate says. "If I hadn't been kind enough to come out to you at this unearthly hour, you'd have gone straight to hospital – standard procedure. And I wouldn't have come, if Jill hadn't phoned me personally. She and my mum are old friends. But don't worry, I'm a proper paid-up doctor, so let's see how you're doing."

Everybody leaves the room as if she's waved a magic wand. "Right, how are you?" she asks shaking down a thermometer. She touches my nose. "Good, no frostbite." She smiles. "Got to stick this under your sweaty armpit."

I don't resist, there's no point. "Don't you like football?" she asks suddenly. Then she watches me, waiting for a reply. "Hmm," she says. "Jill tells me you don't say much. In fact, I don't think she's heard you speak. Isn't that a little inconvenient?"

I don't answer. She purses her lips. We sit in silence until she takes the thermometer out. "Guess what? You're alive," she says.

I glare at her. She leans back and I can tell she's thinking hard about what to say, choosing her words carefully.

When she speaks her voice is clear and direct. "David, we don't know each other yet but I want to tell you something. Whatever rotten deal you've had, you've fallen on your feet here. Jill and Eric are two of the nicest, kindest people I've ever met. Trust them, they won't let you down."

She smiles at me. I frown. A knock comes on the door and Jill asks whether she can come in.

"He's fine," Kate tells her. "Give him a warm drink, put a hot-water bottle in his bed and he'll sleep like a log."

I heave a sigh of relief. They're going to let me stay here. That's good, even if it's just for tonight. I hope they all disappear soon so I can snuggle up with Griffy, fall into a deep, deep sleep and forget. Forget that today was a flat-out disaster. Forget I messed everything up. Forget I'm nothing but a stupid, useless coward. They'll probably take me somewhere tomorrow, lock me up in some place where they can keep an eye on me, but for now I'm OK.

Sergeant Gardner and the social worker come back into the room. Gardner looks dead serious. I lean back on the sofa cushions and close my eyes.

118

"David, we need to talk," Gardner says. "You have to answer some serious questions."

Jill whispers something and there's a general muttering. Then Sergeant Gardner speaks clearly.

"We'll postpone the interview till the morning, you need to rest. You're lucky, despite all the upset you've caused, Jill and Eric want to give you another chance. You'll be able to sleep in your own room tonight." She pauses and clears her throat. "But we can't have you running away again. You'll have to promise not to leave the house. Can you do that?"

I sit still.

She tries again. "David, this is serious. If you don't cooperate, I can't help you."

I open my eyes and look at her. She looks at me. For a few seconds our eyes are locked. Then I nod.

"Not good enough," she says.

I look at Jill. Her eyes plead with me.

I breathe deeply and close my eyes. "Yes," I whisper.

twelve

A telephone is ringing. It rings and rings. Jill shouts from somewhere downstairs. The phone stops then starts up again. Why doesn't she answer it?

Footsteps on the stairs, a knock on the door. Jill comes in with a tray. "Oh good, you're awake. How're you feeling?"

I rub my eyes and squint up at her. The pattern on her jumper glares.

"Here you are, tea and toast. Get up when you're ready. A bath might be a good idea." She puts the tray down on the bedside table. Her eyes roam over me, her mouth opens, closes. She hesitates, uncertain, something left unsaid.

Downstairs, the phone rings again. Jill glances towards the door looking annoyed. "That blessed phone, ringing and ringing, but when I answer – nobody's there. It's a bit unnerving."

She hurries out. I stare after her. Stare at the empty doorway, the white chest of drawers, the yellow teddy bear, his one eye glinting.

The phone stops. I sigh and let my head loll back on the pillow. My legs feel stiff, my body's heavy, I sink into the mattress like a dead whale. Yesterday was the pits. I messed up from beginning to end, it was horrible, I don't want to even think about it. If the scuds hadn't found me I'd be dead or in hospital – could have ended up on a trolley next to Tiny. I suppose I should be glad I'm safe but I can't rest, knowing he's out there. I've got to make another plan, a better one, nothing left to chance – have to be patient, give myself time to track Him down – then, strike!

I sit up and reach for the tray. It's carefully laid, everything matching, blue and white plate, blue cup, white saucer, toast cut into neat triangles. It's like a ruddy still-life painting. I don't know why but it really irritates me, my head aches at the sight of it. I pick up a piece of toast and aim at the teddy bear. Splat! Take that! I sit up and the remaining toast scatters, one piece drops to the floor and when I get out of bed, I mash it under my heel.

Bloody breakfast in bed. Why are they treating me so well? They should shout at me, go apeshit, say what they really think. Instead they bring me bloody breakfast in bed like I'm a friggin' invalid. I hate it. I can't stand this house; everything calm, everything planned, everything in order. What am I doing here? The scuds should have left me, I should be on the streets.

I shrug off my idiot pyjamas, throw them across the room, then seize a drawer handle and pull. Socks and underwear spill on to the floor. Ruffling through, I find a pair of boxers and dance round to pull them up one-handed. I'm bending down to pick up some socks when my head jerks as if I've been hit. Mum's voice fills my head.

David, look what you're doing to yourself . So angry, so unhappy. Let it go. Find some peace.

Tears start pricking at my eyes. Oh no you don't, Mum. You can't talk me into changing my mind. I won't listen. I jump up and down, shaking my head.

This is a good place, David, they're giving you a chance to make a new life here. Don't throw it away.

I clap my hands over my ears. You don't understand, Mum, I'm suffocating.

A new plan, that's what I need. Frantically, I pull open the desk drawer and reach for paper. No! No time for that. Plan in your head, your stupid head.

Downstairs, the phone's ringing again. It rings and rings then I hear the answer machine cut in.

I slam the desk drawer shut and bang my fist on the handle. Where's he gone? Where did he go last night? He's hiding somewhere or somebody's hiding him. The scuds haven't found him or they'd be back to question me. I've got to get to him quick.

David, David, you promised you wouldn't run away again.

Tough. Some promises are made to be broken. They should have had more sense than trust me.

I hum, to blot out Mum's voice. I hum as I haul out my bag, I hum louder when I hear footsteps coming up the stairs. Hum, hum. I push the bag back under the bed just before Eric pokes his head round the door.

"Ah, good, you sound brighter. Can I have a chat with you before Sarah arrives?"

He says it softly but his tone is serious. I turn away.

"I'll be down in the kitchen, David. Don't be long."

Well make your mind up. First Jill tells me to have a bath and now you're telling me to hurry downstairs. I don't want to sit in the kitchen with you asking questions I'm not going to answer – just the thought of it makes me squirm. And if Miss Happy Clappy, all smiling I know what's best for you Social Waster turns up, I'll be sick. Then there's Gardner; after last night when she made me promise, actually heard me speak – she'll think she's on to some kind of breakthrough, probably imagines I'm ready to pour my heart out. So it won't be long before she's knocking on the door. I've got to think fast.

Big problem – my brain seems to have turned to porridge. I can't think of any clear plan. I wander into the bathroom, have a pee and clean my teeth. I'm washing my hands when I see a big bottle of bath oil.

Suddenly, the urge to lock the door and shut everything and everybody out takes over. Sod 'em all.

I lean over, drop the plug into the bath, turn the taps on and pour in a big dollop of syrupy green oil. The hot water goes cloudy and throws up clusters of rainbow bubbles.

He'll be living in Derby – must be. That's why he was waiting for Steve and Tiny – he was waiting for a lift home. Did bugger all to help them though, watched them being beat up and carted away. His best mates! Typical – he gets off on beating women, but hasn't got the guts for a real fight.

I hear a door bang downstairs. Quickly I pull off my clothes and get into the water. They can bang all they like, I'm not coming out.

My knees are sticking up like mountains in snow. I scoop up piles of foam and cover them. I try to think myself into his head. Gran would be his best bet. She always stuck up for him even when she knew he was belting Mum. Hideous old bat! But if he's staying with Gran, how's he avoided detection? The scuds must have searched her house.

The bubbles are going cold, they lie shivering on top of my knees. I lower my legs and run in some more hot water. If I were him, what would I do? Where would I go?

Somebody's shouting my name. I turn on the hot tap, lie back and enjoy the warmth. I'll come out when

I'm ready. As soon as I've thought up a new plan.

In the kitchen, Eric's reading the paper. I'm halfway through the door when he looks up.

"Ah, David." He peers at me over the top of a giant-sized page. I stand still, head down. "Come on in." He puts the paper down and gestures for me to come forward. He pulls out a chair. "Here, sit down. I'm reading about yesterday's match. Big headlines. Not bad for a little division-two club, eh? Look."

He turns the paper towards me. CHESTERFIELD SLAUGHTER BLEATING RAMS. "Says David Reeves was man of the match. Leeds are after him. Chesterfield won't hang on to him for long. Pity you missed his third goal." He glances at me. "I saw it just before I realized you weren't coming back, before it finally sunk in you'd gone."

I look down at the paper. There's a photo of a player in mid-air and the ball heading for the top corner of the net.

"It was a great goal," Eric says.

I bite my lip. I know what's coming.

"David, why did you run off from the match? Where were you going?"

I stare at the picture, it blurs, the ball goes into the net. Eric taps his fingers on the paper. "Is there something we don't know, David? Somewhere you want to go or somebody you want to see?" He squints at me, his eyes narrowing. "Is it us, David? Perhaps we're not right for you. You don't want to stay here? If you talk to us, you could help us understand."

The photo's in focus again, the player for ever frozen in mid-air. Eric folds the paper and puts it down, then he stretches his hands towards me, palms upwards until they're nearly touching my knees. "You've got to give us a chance to help you, David. Come out of that shell."

I say nothing.

He watches me closely. "David, why were you carrying that knife?"

After a few seconds, he sighs, makes fists of his hands and bangs them gently, rhythmically, on his knees. Out in the hall the telephone rings.

"That damn phone. It's been going all morning but when we answer nobody's there. Somebody's playing tricks."

It carries on ringing from the hall, shrill and desperate. Eric gets up and goes out. When he comes back he's pulling on a jacket.

"Well, at least somebody was there this time. It was Jill phoning from the supermarket. For some reason her credit card won't work so she's standing there with a trolley full of stuff and no means of paying. I'll pop down with some money, only be a few minutes, Sarah's on her way here, so. . ." His arms drop to his sides. "We've got to be able to trust you. I can trust you, can't I?"

He looks at me, our eyes meet, he nods and starts to walk out into the hallway. "Sarah will be here any minute so let her in." He pauses, half turns. "Talk to her. You might like her if you give her a chance."

As soon as I hear the car start up I zoom out into the hall. I'm halfway up the stairs when the phone starts ringing. I stop, hesitate, then decide to ignore it. My foot goes up on to the next step. Somehow the tone sharpens, seems more shrill, grows louder. I turn round, run down and grab the receiver.

I don't say who I am. I don't speak but I hear somebody on the other end. I hear a sigh and breathing, then there's a voice. My stomach clenches tight as a fist, my breath mists the plastic. It's like a voice from outer space, alien, disembodied but oh, so familiar.

"Davey, Davey, is that you?"

I drop the phone and race upstairs, fall into my room and slam the door shut. Rushing over to the window I scan the back lawn, the shrubs and fences. What do I expect? To see his grinning head peering over? I bash my head against the glass and then I turn and dive on to the bed. How's he found me?

Safe, I thought I was safe here. There was no way for him to know where I was. Even though he spotted me last night, how's he know where I live?

I slam my fist into the bedhead, my broken arm zings. I feel sick with pain but I leap up and dive for my bag. I've got to clear out. If I stay he'll come and get me.

He's done it before in the dead of night, dragged me from my bed. The memory of that screaming night sends my breath spurting into my throat.

I'm throwing stuff into my bag when I hear the knock, a sharp rap on the front door. My heart thumps, slams up against my ribs so hard I gasp and drop the bag. Two knocks now, loud and clear. A shout. Not Him, thank God not Him.

"Hello," a voice in the hall.

Footsteps coming up the stairs – she must have let herself in, nosey cow. I kick the bag back under the bed.

"David."

I stand still holding my breath.

"David? You in there?"

Go away, stupid bitch. Go away.

"David, are you going to let me in?"

Sod off, sod off.

The door opens slowly and she peers round, head without a body, green eyes glinting, features sharp as a witch.

"Jill said you'd be up here."

I glare.

"How are you?"

I glare harder, gritting my teeth, snorting down my nose. She moves into the room.

"It's a nice room this. Good to have your own room, isn't it?"

She's ignoring the mess, stepping over scattered

clothing and mashed toast. I glare at her. *I don't want you in here, so piss off.*

She ignores my dead eye and without invitation comes over and sits on the bed. "So there's a problem."

I sigh and look away. *Yes, Miss bloody Social Weasel, there's a problem. Somebody told Him where I am.*

She straightens my duvet. What gives her the right?

"Will you tell me why you ran away from the football match yesterday?"

I chew my bottom lip.

"And why you had a knife in your pocket?"

She runs her hand down the duvet cover, bends to pick up the mashed toast and return it to the plate. Then she raises her head and looks at me. Her smile has fallen off her face. We look at each other and its like she's seeing me for the first time. "Come and sit down, David."

I do as I'm told but only because it suits me. I want to hear what she's got to say. What lies she'll tell.

"OK. We've got to get things sorted out. I'll tell you my position, no bullshit, right?"

Oh, yes, no bullshit, please. Just tell me who told Him where I was. You? Or was it the stupid squealing scuds?

She's looking at me again. "Here's the deal. It's my job to put you in a safe place and make sure you're being properly cared for. I've done that so that's a big part of my job sorted. But if you keep running away, we'll have to re-think. Then there's other stuff.

School – you've got to attend. Health – we've got to get that arm better. And then there's communication – or lack of it on your part. Not speaking presents particular difficulties. We may need to get professional help."

I bite my lip and turn away. Why doesn't she get to the good part, the part where she says He's coming for me?

"David," she says sharply. "Don't throw away the best chance you've got. We all care about you. I can't make any promises but I can say if you make an effort and talk to Jill and Eric they'll be willing to have you here for quite a while. Surely that's better than being switched from place to place. They want to look after you and, you need a home."

I look at her sitting there smug as a cat, her green eyes glowing like she's offering me a treat. I stare and I feel anger rising and swelling till my stomach and throat are on fire. I try to swallow, to push it down but I can't.

"You told Him where I was!"

My voice sounds like an earthquake. Her eyes flicker, bulge and stare.

"No. . . David," she stammers, shaking her head.

"He spoke to me," I shout. "He knows I'm here."

She moves closer to me. "Who do you mean, David? Your dad?"

"He's not my dad."

She starts asking questions, digging and prying. I turn away; I've said too much already. I've done with her. I get up and move over to the window. She follows like a bad smell, asking when he spoke to me, was he at the football match, was that why I ran? Questions, questions, but I'm not saying any more. She can't help. Talk, talk, talk, words are useless. Action, that's what's needed. Action and I'll do it. I'm the action man. The hit man, David.

She tries to put her hand on my shoulder and turn me towards her but I shrug her off. Downstairs I hear Jill and Eric arrive, Griffy barks. I turn to face the wall.

Miss SW, call me Sarah, hovers, then says, "I'm going to have a quick word with Jill and Eric. Think about what I've said, David. Trust me."

I don't move as she goes out. I sit completely still for a few seconds, then I pull out my bag. This time nothing will stop me.

thirteen

Softly, softly, step by step, I slide along the landing. My bag's on my shoulder, my coat's under my arm. I feel my way forward, testing the floor, not wanting to make a sound.

At the top of the stairs I stop, startled by raised voices. I gulp and tense; hear the loud scrape of a chair below. My foot hovers over the top step, my anorak rustles against the banister. Any moment, Jill will come bombing up the stairs to find me. I should go back, wait till it gets dark. I'm on the point of turning round, slipping back to my room when the kitchen door slams; the voices are drowned.

Swift as a shadow, I'm down the stairs, flash past the kitchen, into the hallway and – oh damn, Griffy's lying there – she gets up and comes to me, tail wagging.

Stay, Griffy, stay.

I open the front door and try to pull my bag through

without her escaping. I don't succeed. I end up on the outside, Griffy with me. She cocks her head, raises a paw and looks at me expectantly, waiting for the magic word. For a split-second I hesitate, weighing, debating, then I lean down and whisper.

Half-running, half-staggering, my big sports bag bouncing against my shin, I flee up the street, Griffy leaping with excitement. She isn't on a lead, so I struggle to keep up with her, anxious in case she dashes ahead. Between breaths I mutter, "Heel, Griffy, heel," – and she almost obeys.

When I'm round the corner I stop. I daren't risk it any longer, there's a lot of traffic on the main road and I don't want her to scoot under a car. I stop and tell her to sit while I unzip my bag and scrummage inside. My hand finds a belt which I slip through her collar. Precious moments wasted but it's worth it, now she's safe. I give a quick glance over my shoulder and plough on.

Griffy seems to have decided where we're going, she tugs me uphill, away from town. I let her lead and somehow manage to hold on to her, the belt and my heavy bag, clutched in one hand. Thankfully, after a few metres she stops. I bend down and pat her. "Good girl."

She's brought me to a bus stop. Fine by me; any bus will do, as long as I get clear of this place. I just hope one comes along soon because the bus shelter provides no shelter – it's glass and I'm framed inside, obvious as a boil on a backside.

I scan the road. A green car's coming; nowhere to hide. I turn my back. Genius! So Jill's not going to recognize the dog? Thankfully the car sails past, others follow behind, then miracle of miracles, a red bus appears.

I lurch to the edge of the pavement and stick out my pot arm. On the front of the bus it says MATLOCK. Soon as the door opens Griffy leaps forward and rushes up the steps as if she's a regular.

"One to Matlock," I say, though I've no idea where Matlock is.

The bus driver gives me a hard look. "That your dog?"

I gulp. "Er . . . yes."

"Two halves then?" he says.

I frown.

"The dog," he says.

Light dawns. "Oh, I. . . I didn't know you had to pay for dogs."

"Well, you do."

He stares at me and for a moment I think he's going to throw us off, then his face relaxes. "Oh, go on," he says. "Give me a pound, that'll do."

I hand over the coin and struggle down the aisle, my bag thumping against every seat. An old woman with pink hair stares at me; a man holding a big bunch of flowers sits whistling.

134

Griffy pulls me to the back seat and flops down. It takes me longer to relax. My breath is snorting down my nose like I've just run a marathon, my insides are break-dancing and my arm is on fire. And the bus doesn't help; it sways like a roller coaster as it rattles up the main road, before turning sharp left and jolting slowly through a housing estate. I wish it would get a move on, I'd feel better if we were out of Chesterfield. We seem to be slowing at every stop even though nobody's waiting to get on. Then, when we're opposite another bus, our driver stops and leans out of the window chatting to the other driver. Come on, we're holding up the traffic. He doesn't seem to care though; he shouts and laughs like he's in a pub, until finally, he closes the window and revs the engine.

Driving past an ugly old brick church, we turn left again and back on to the main road. The engine groans as we labour up a steep hill and then, at last we leave the houses behind and drive into the countryside.

I lean on my bag and feel a shiver of excitement – I've escaped. I check the back window. No green car following and every jolt of the bus is taking me further away from Chesterfield. When we reach the top of the hill I look down triumphantly on acres of green fields. Now I can begin my quest.

Travelling higher we pass over moorland where a fierce wind bends dark trees. In the middle of a field a girl on horseback is circling round and round; down a gravel driveway is a windmill someone has converted into a house. My stomach twists as I wonder where I'll sleep tonight.

Griffy is wriggling under the seat, making snuffling noises. I guess she's found something to eat and my mind leaps ahead. How am I going to feed her? I haven't got enough money to feed myself, never mind a dog as well. I shouldn't have brought her, she's too much of a responsibility. I'm an idiot. I should be plotting my next move, not worrying about feeding dogs. She squirms backwards, her shaggy bum pushing against my knee. When she turns round, her nose is stuck in a crisp packet. Daft dog.

The man holding the flowers starts to sing, "Fly me to the Moon". Griffy gives the crisp packet a last lick, drops it and leans her head on my knee. I stroke her, rubbing gently behind her ears. We'll do Him, eh Griffy, you and me? Together. We'll find Gran's house, lie in wait and when we're ready, we'll pounce.

I shift my foot on the last word. Griffy looks up at me and wags her tail. I doubt if she could harm anybody.

The bus sways lazily, rhythmically: stop, start, stop, start. A few more people get on, the flower man gets off, still singing. I doze, my head lolling like a loose turnip.

Next time I'm fully awake we're heading down a steep hill between dark stone buildings. Matlock, I guess. Good, should be safe here, nobody looking for me. Now, let's hope I can get to Derby without being spotted.

As soon as the bus stops, Griffy's raring to go. I hardly have a chance to grab my bag before she's pulling me along the aisle and down the steps. I jump down into a cold, grotty concrete building. Our bus is the only one there, it doesn't look good for getting to Derby. I approach an old man holding some carrier bags.

"No, nothing to Derby here," he says. "Go and stand in bus bay out front. You'll do better there."

I go outside where some people are waiting.

"You've just missed one," a woman tells me. "You'll have to wait an hour for the next."

I don't want to stand and wait all that time, and I'm thirsty, so I wander off in search of a drink. The doors of a supermarket slide open but a woman in uniform tells me dogs can't go inside. I back away and hurry across the pelican crossing to a newsagent's. I tell Griffy to heel and she seems to understand, sliding quietly into the shop at the back of my legs. The man behind the counter gives us a glance but doesn't say anything.

They've got sweets in jars, chocolate and crisps as well as newspapers but what I'm looking for is a drink. I circle a display of birthday cards and see a fridge in the corner. Just as I'm about to open the door, a glass case on the wall catches my eye – it's full of knives, blades of every description. If only the bloody scuds hadn't taken mine. How am I going to get another? I'll have to steal one.

I buy a carton of orange and walk out into the street, follow a little boy in a red anorak; his mum's pulling him along telling him to hurry. They turn into a car park where there's a sign for a railway station.

An hour later I jump down on to a platform at Derby station. My luck was in; I didn't have to wait long for a train. So, without much trouble at all, I'm here, right where I wanted to be.

Following the other passengers up a long flight of steps I keep my eyes peeled, the scuds might be watching out for me. A boy with a broken arm and a dog, too obvious; it's going to be difficult to hide.

At the top of the steps I climb on to a walkway which stretches over the platforms. People hurry past as I bump along to the end where there's another lot of steps leading down to a big entrance hall. I drop my bag and lean over a rail, scanning the scene below. Travellers with backpacks and cases, bags and umbrellas are arriving, meeting and leaving. Light glares up at me glancing off the marble floor. Wide glass doors lead to the street. Outside, I can see parked cars and taxis but I won't be leaving yet – standing guard at the entrance are two scuds.

I dodge back. Griffy senses my fear and tucks in close. When I turn and look behind me, all I see at the far end of the walkway is a blank concrete wall. No way out.

Backtracking, I frantically search for another exit but all I find are more platforms. I'm feeling tired and desperate when I finally end up back at the top of the same steps I climbed earlier. Glumly, I put my bag down and stare at the train and tracks beneath. I don't know what I'm going to do, perhaps I'll just have to wait, sit it out till the scuds leave, but I'm losing precious hours of daylight. I want to suss out Gran's place before it gets dark.

I slump back against the wall and curse. I'm cold and hungry, a sharp wind's blowing down the walkway and I huddle into my coat. I kick at a cigarette packet, sending it skidding across the concrete and down the steps. My eyes follow its path and I see an old lady surfacing. She's struggling up the steps with a heavy suitcase, puffing and panting, looking fit to collapse. Even as I'm thinking, "poor old thing", an idea pops into my head.

When she reaches the top, I step forward. "Excuse me. Can I carry that for you?"

She glances at me and puts the case down. Her breath is whooshing in and out, loud as an air pump, a film of sweat glistens on her forehead and her cheeks are fiery red.

I wait while she puffs a bit more then she says, "It's very kind of you dear, but you look as if you've got enough to cope with."

It's true. A pot arm, a bag and a dog, but my mind's whirring fast.

"No, it's all right," I say. "Look, if you hold my dog. I'll carry your case."

"Are you sure?"

"Yep." Putting my bag on my shoulder I hand her the belt attached to Griffy. "Don't worry, she won't pull."

I pick up her suitcase with my good hand; it's heavy but I can just about manage it. I hope I'm right about Griffy, I'm relying on her not to catapult the poor woman head over heels down the stairs.

"Not many young people would offer," the old lady says. She trots along behind me still breathing heavily. "It's very kind of you. Some people nearly knocked me over as they rushed past."

I can't answer because now I'm panting and my arm is killing me. At the top of the stairs leading down to the entrance hall, I stop. "Just a sec," I say. I drop the case and quickly unzip my bag, pulling out my anorak. I put my bag on my left shoulder and loop my anorak through the strap so it hangs over my plastered arm. "More comfortable now," I say, trying to smile.

We walk down the steps together, a boy, his granny and her dog. I try to walk calmly, blend into the surroundings, but the case is so heavy I lurch sideways a couple of times. Thank goodness Griffy's behaving herself. Some people below look up but we don't seem to be attracting much attention and best of all, there's no sign of the scuds.

At the bottom of the steps the old lady stops and opens her handbag. "Thank you so much," she says. "Here, let me give you something for your trouble."

Over her shoulder I catch sight of the scuds approaching.

"No, I don't want anything," I say. "I was happy to help." I try frantically to think of something else to say. "Erm, is anybody meeting you?"

"No." She shakes her head. "I'll get a taxi outside."

"I'll carry the case outside for you, then," I say.

The woman hesitates. "Are you sure? Won't somebody be waiting for you?"

"No, it's all right."

The scuds are closing in. I step closer to the lady and pick up the case. "My mum just died," I say. "I'm coming to live with my dad but he's—"

Before I can finish, she makes a sort of "Oh, how terrible" sound and puts her hand on my shoulder. "You poor thing," she says, patting me over and over.

I lean towards her. Mum, forgive me. I feel like a traitor, but when I see the scuds turning away, I feel a surge of triumph.

"Let's find you a taxi," the woman says. "Come on. I'm not having you getting lost. What's your dad's address?"

Together we walk out of the station. Granny holding

her grandson's arm, a black dog trotting by their side. Out of the corner of my eye I see the scuds have split up, one of them's talking to a boy about my age. I almost smile.

"I hope things turn out well with your dad," the old woman says. "Here, look, if you ever want somebody to talk to, my name and telephone number are on there." She hands me a gold address label stuck on a bit of paper. EVIE AND DENNIS THORNTON. "We had them done for Christmas cards but not long after, Dennis passed away. The address and phone number are still the same though. I didn't want to move."

"Thank you," I say.

"Now, here's a taxi. Where did you say your dad lives, dear?"

"Pilot Street," I say.

She opens the taxi door for me and before I can protest, Griffy jumps in. Well, I guess it'll cut down on walking. I follow and stuff my bag on to the seat. The woman leans in and pushes a five pound note in my hand. "That's for your taxi fare. I couldn't rest if I thought you hadn't got home safely."

She waves as the taxi pulls away and I'm off to Pilot Street, Gran's house, his mother – if she still lives there.

I look out of the window, nothing looks familiar. It's a long time since I was here. When me and Mum left Him the first time we lived in Mum's friend's house, but we had to leave cos he broke in and smashed stuff.

Next time we went to the shelter in Sheffield and then two more places before we got the house in Chesterfield. It was a new start for us but he found us, he always found us in the end.

I look out at the tall buildings pressed together, shops, offices, a new space-age football stadium, then terraced houses, some boarded up, some with grubby curtains, some neat and brightly painted. Mum hated Derby.

As the taxi lurches, Griffy slips around on the shiny seat, mouth open, tongue poking out. When we stop at traffic lights, she stands up.

"Down, Griffy."

She moves closer to me and puts a paw on my leg. I stroke her dusty coat, smooth back the long bits over her eyes and hold her steady as the taxi pulls away again.

"What number?" the taxi driver yells over his shoulder.

I don't know.

"Pilot Street. What number?" he yells again.

I haven't a clue.

"The address?" he yells even louder as if he's talking to a foreigner.

"Sixty two," I shout back, hoping there is one.

We weave up and down narrow streets. There're a lot of Indian shops. An old man with a turban and long white beard stands and stares as we pass. Some women

143

wearing dresses bright as butterflies are in a huddle, talking. Then we turn a corner and the taxi slows.

"Which end of the street is it?"

"Next to that one with the red door."

When I've paid I get out and pretend to walk up to the house. It isn't 62, it's got a number 46 on it, but the taxi driver doesn't care – package delivered, he's on his way. All houses look the same. I don't remember which house it is and I haven't got a clue about what I'm going to do next.

fourteen

What do I do now? Knock on all the doors in Pilot Street till I find Gran? She might not even live here any more. I curse myself because I can't remember the number of the house. I ought to, he used to drag me here every time he had to take care of me. One time when he'd put Mum in hospital, he brought me here to Gran's while he went out boozing, came back in the middle of the night, drunk and shouting. Gran threatened to throw a bucket of water over him.

I remember looking down from the window, seeing a dark figure staggering in the middle of the street, swearing. I must have been in the front bedroom. There were orange curtains and the window frame was painted dark red, the colour of blood.

I look up and down the street but can't see any house with orange curtains; the front doors are all colours but not one is blood-red. I walk slowly past them until I reach the end of the street. When I look back, it's hard to tell which is the top and which is the bottom. But when I look across the road and see a school, memories come flooding back.

Tall spiked railings enclose the playground. Shrill voices wafting on the wind. A girl with her face squashed between two iron rails stares with goggle eyes at Mum and me as we walk past. I ask Mum, are the railings to keep children in or out? She laughs and swings my hand as we wait to cross the road. Then pumping my arm in time to the rhythm she sings: "You put the children in, You put the children out, In, out, In, out, Shake them all about." I join in and we carry on singing as we cross the road and walk up the street.

How many steps did we take before we reached Gran's house? I don't know. Perhaps if I cross the road and start from the school it might jog my memory.

I wait while a sudden stream of cars whizzes past. But I'm not really seeing the cars, I'm still thinking about Mum, hearing her high, clear, singing voice. Behind me a door clicks open making me jump. I turn to see two women step out on to the pavement, one with a big brown shopping bag and the other holding the hand of a small boy. They stare at me, their eyes like big, brown beans. When they've gone past the little boy cranes his head to see me and nearly trips. His mum yanks him forwards shouting at him in a foreign language.

Well, that's one house Gran definitely doesn't live in. I'm just about to cross the road when I hear shouting. My heart sinks as I see a group of kids approaching and I shrink back against the brick wall of the house behind me. One of the kids is walking half on, half off the pavement, hands in pockets looking like he owns the street; another's kicking a football – they spell trouble. I look up and down the street anxiously as if I'm waiting for someone.

A little kid in big trainers comes close. He stops and glares at Griffy who's flopped down on the pavement again.

"That your dog?" he asks.

I nod, hoping he'll clear off. I expect him to say something clever but he looks suddenly nervous and shy. "Can I stroke her?" he asks, hesitantly.

I shrug. "Yeah, if you like."

"Will she bite?"

"No."

He takes a couple of steps forward and bends down to stroke Griffy. The rest of the kids follow suit. I'm nervous in case they're rough with her but they pat her gently. Of course, Griffy does her usual thing, rolling over and putting her legs in the air.

"Look," the kid says. "She likes us." He stands up. "Wish I had a dog," he says longingly.

"Yeah," I say. "She's a great dog."

He seems a friendly kid so I'm just about to ask him

if he knows where Mrs Dawson lives when he says, "See ya," and dashes off, the others following.

I watch them disappear down the street. I wish I could go with them. I'm no footballer but I wouldn't mind a kick about on the park with some mates, maybe go to a chippy afterwards, then run home to watch TV.

It's getting colder and the light's fading. My plan to find Him seemed simple enough – watch and wait – but there's nowhere to hide, the windows look out on to the street and if I stand here much longer, people are bound to get suspicious. I can't sleep on the street and I'm hungry. I wish I'd eaten the breakfast Jill brought me this morning. Was it only this morning? It seems like days ago.

Now it's beginning to rain, just a slight drizzle but it's the sort of rain that wets you through. I pick up my bag and start to move off to find shelter but I hear something. A car engine, a throaty, rattling roar followed by the explosion of exhaust. It appears a moment later, rolling round the corner, and silver fog lamps glinting. I can't believe it. The scuds reckoned he'd disappeared – it's taken me just a few hours to find him.

I drop my head as he passes. I hear my heart thumping, Griffy stands and nuzzles at the back of my knees. The car explodes up the street before it gives a final pop and stops at the kerb.

I rush towards it, planning to take him by surprise. *Bang*, get him, before he sees me. Automatically my hand goes to my pocket but there's no knife. I don't know how I'm going to hurt him but somehow I will. I'm hurrying now. Quick, long steps. The car door's opening. I drop Griffy's lead. There's two or three metres between us. The car door swings back, the driver's getting out, the door slams shut.

"Gran!"

The name shoots out before I can stop it. The woman looks at me, puzzled. She doesn't know me, but I'd know that pinched potato face anywhere. Her eyes dart all over me, there's a gleam of recognition.

"Davey, Davey, is it you?"

I'm standing with my fist raised ready for action but my mouth gapes open in surprise. She steps closer, my fingers clench, then loosen, and my hand drops. I should run away, clear out, but I'm so nervous I can't move. I gulp and swallow, heave a big shuddering sigh and then I say the first daft thing that comes into my head, "I never knew you could drive."

Gran arches her thin eyebrows; purses her mouth. For a moment she looks annoyed, then her face smears with a slow smile. She points a bony finger at me and gives a triumphant chuckle as if she's just won at Bingo. "Well I never! It is Davey, isn't it?"

I can't answer. This isn't what was supposed to happen. It's all gone wrong.

The smile on Gran's face grows. "Well, well, fancy seeing you here. Hmm, you've grown, still a skinny

149

little stick though, aren't you? And what have you done to your arm?"

My eyes glaze over – her face blurs, she grows two heads. I sway slightly and she catches my arm. "You'd better come inside, you don't look well."

I lean against the brick wall while she finds her key. When I follow her inside, the house is cold and smells of cigarettes.

She switches on a light. "Come through," she shouts and I stumble along the back of a sofa, round a big chair and into the kitchen.

"Well, this is a surprise," Gran says. Then she looks down at Griffy. "Where's the dog from? Is it all right?"

I nod. I can't speak. Memories flood into my head stabbing me like fire. Him shouting, Mum turning round, a sharp ripping sound. He's standing in the middle of the kitchen, a surprised look on his face, the sleeve of Mum's blouse dangling from his fingers. He shouts it's her fault, all her bloody fault, then he snaps into action using the sleeve like a whip, slashing at Mum's face. When this doesn't hurt her enough he follows up with slaps and punches. I try to get to her but somebody's holding me back. I scream and kick out. My legs are slapped.

Later, when everything's quiet, I look for Mum, but she's gone, I can't find her anywhere. At the table I climb on to a chair, put my finger into a spot of blood, it's dried to a crust.

"Thought you'd gone to live with a family. That's

what I was told when I asked." Gran looks at me quickly, then her eyes slide away. "I did ask," she mutters. "I did want to look after you, Davey."

She shrugs off her coat. "Sit down. I'll make a cup of tea."

I feel like a soldier who's crossed the enemy line. Sitting on the edge of a chair, I lean my elbow on the table, trying to remember what happened that day, where Mum went, who looked after me. Did she come back because of me?

"If you've come to find your dad, I can't help you," Gran says. "He left me his car two weeks ago and I haven't seen hide nor hair of him since."

I swallow hard and pat Griffy's head. "It's a sad business," she says, as she runs water into the kettle.

A sad business because he's disappeared or is she actually feeling sad about Mum? She plugs in the kettle, finds some mugs then sits down.

"Shaken, he was, shaken to bits," she says. "Came to my door, pale as a ghost. Right upset. I know he didn't always see eye to eye with her but he loved her. He'd never have wished that on her."

I bite my lip so hard I can taste blood. I want to snatch up a mug and smash it into her head. She's tapping out a cigarette, pinches one in her thin yellow fingers and lights up. Taking a long first drag she sighs and then as she puffs out, attempts a smile. "Well, I expect you could stay with your old Gran, eh? Don't

151

want to be with strangers at a time like this, do you?" The smile becomes a sly grin. "We could 'elp each other," she says.

I wonder what she has in mind. She reaches for an ashtray. "Not sure I could keep a dog though. It'll have to go back to where it came from."

Griffy gets up as if her name's been called and goes to sit next to Gran, putting a paw on her knee.

Gran looks down at her and sniffs. "Hmm, we'll see, she seems well trained."

I'm eating a bowl of tomato soup when the phone rings. Gran gets up, looking anxious. Her voice is sharp. "Who is this?" She waits, breathing into the mouthpiece. "No, he's not here. I haven't seen him."

She listens again. Somebody's giving her an earful.

"No, I won't get in touch with you. Why should I? When I said he could come here to live I wasn't good enough, you didn't give me the time of day. Well, you can get lost."

She purses her lips as she slams down the phone. "Bloody Social Services poking their noses in wanting to know if I'd seen you. Does that dog need to go out? She's looking a bit shifty."

I shake my head.

"Don't say much, do you?"

I spoon in the last mouthful of soup and give Griffy a piece of bread.

"Shouldn't feed dogs at the table, makes 'em beg," she says. But then she opens the fridge and pulls out a plate with a bone on it. "She can have this in a minute. It's only knuckle end, all I can afford."

She opens a drawer, pulls out a carving knife and chops off a few slices. "There, that'll do me for a sandwich."

Griffy is her friend for life, her tail wags as she munches on the bone. I get up and take my dirty dishes to the sink. While I'm washing them I take the opportunity to pick up the meat knife and slide it up my sleeve.

When I turn round Gran's jotting something down on a piece of paper.

"Gran," I say. "Do you have any idea where Dad might be?" I nearly choke on the three-letter word but it's got to be said.

She gives me a long hard look. "Why do you want to know?"

I steel myself. "I miss him," I say.

Gran's eyes narrow. "You were never close," she says.

"It's different now," I say.

"Hmm." She sucks on her cigarette and looks thoughtful as if she's weighing something up. "You sure you weren't followed here?" she asks.

I shake my head. "Nobody knew I was coming here," I say.

She's still looking uncertain, as if she knows something but won't tell. When she speaks her voice is sharp. "He hasn't bothered to take me into his confidence. I don't understand why he's seen fit to do a disappearing act." She blows out a circle of smoke. "It's not like he's done anything wrong. It was an accident, wasn't it?"

There's a flicker of doubt in her eyes. I swallow hard, look at her and nod.

fifteen

"Well, we'd better think about where you're going to sleep tonight. I got your dad's things stuffed in the back bedroom so you can't go in there," Gran says sharply.

She gives a loud sigh as if I'm causing a lot of trouble then she goes out of the room. I hear her climbing the stairs. Swift as water, I shift over to where I dumped my bag. Bending down, I unzip the bag and jiggle the stolen carving knife from my sleeve. After a quick glance at the door, I thrust the knife between my clothes and zip the bag up tight.

Gran's footsteps pause. She shouts down the stairs. "You could go in the front room. I don't sleep in there no more cos of the noise." She waits a moment. "Come on. I'm not sorting this out by myself."

She's standing on the landing. "Don't let that dog come up," she orders.

Griffy's one step behind me. "Down Griffy," I say

hopefully. To my surprise, she wags her tail and obeys, retracing her steps and flopping at the bottom of the stairs.

"She's a good dog," Gran says approvingly. "Now, you come in here. We'll make the front bed up."

It's a double bed stuffed into a corner. The room smells damp and on one wall the orange-flowered wallpaper has a brown stain.

"Don't wrinkle your nose up. Everything's clean. I'm sure it's better than a council home any day."

I wait by the window while she pulls back the orange bedspread. Then she turns round. "Move out the way," she orders. "Let me find some sheets."

I step back and stare into the street below. It's raining, a man is pulling a little dog along and two women in bright dresses are getting out of a taxi. For some stupid reason I watch for the boys I saw earlier, they could be returning from the park, I might see them. I look towards the bottom of the street but they don't appear. I press my forehead against the glass, my breath mists the view. Gran comes back with pink striped sheets and two blankets.

"What're you doing at that window? Come away, I've just cleaned those panes." She puts the bedding down on top of the dresser. "These are all I've got to spare, they'll have to do. You should be warm enough." She shakes a sheet over the mattress. "Come on, never mind nosing out the window, grab this corner and help."

It's a bit difficult trying to lift the mattress and tuck the sheet in when I can only use one hand. I do my best but Gran clucks with annoyance and pushes me out of the way. "Go on, I'll do it. You're slower than a council workman."

She makes a big show of flapping and smoothing the blankets and then she straightens up. "Right, that'll do."

It looks good enough to me, I could have been sleeping in a bus shelter.

I wait for her next instructions while she gets a tissue out of her pocket and blows her nose. She sniffs. "Do you miss your mum?" she suddenly blurts out.

The words hit me like a slap in the face. I stand with my mouth half-open, unable to say anything, just staring.

"It must have been difficult living with new people," she says. "Never mind – you're with me now."

I look at a picture on the opposite wall; ducks are flying over a sunlit lake.

Gran's voice cuts in. "Were they in it for the money?"

I don't understand what she means at first, what money? Then it dawns on me.

"They didn't do it for the money," I say.

"Why else would anybody want to look after a stranger's kid?" she asks.

She picks up the bedspread and throws it over the blankets.

"I don't know. Maybe because their own kid died," I say.

"Oh," she says. "You were doing them a favour then."

I blink as tears prick my eyes. She's got no idea about Eric and Jill.

"Well, you're better off with family," she says. "Families should stick together, eh?" She gives me a sharp look, then turns abruptly and goes out of the room.

I wipe my eyes as she clatters downstairs. I wouldn't care if she fell. She's got a nerve, talking about families. If she cared about family, why didn't she try and sort her son out, stop him from belting his wife?

I sit on the edge of the tightly made bed and hear her talking to Griffy. After that I hear her in the kitchen, a cupboard door bangs, a chair scrapes. I don't want to join her, don't want to see her mean pinched face. It's cold up here though, so I lift my bag on to the bed and pull out my fleece. The knife falls from the folds of thick material. I grasp the handle and hold it up, tilting the blade to catch the light. A smear of grease stains the blade. I wipe it on the bedspread.

Just as I'm about to slip the knife back into the bag, I see a corner of Mum's parcel. Without thinking, I grab it, pull it out, hold it to my nose and sniff. Hospitals! It smells of bloody hospitals. I look at the name written on the giant envelope. ALISON DAWSON.

My fingers tremble as I pull the flap open, I hold my breath as I tip the envelope. Mum's red purse comes out first, the zip's broken and the colour's worn off at the corners, inside there's a few coins and a coupon. I tip the envelope again and some beads fall out; letters, papers and more stuff showers down. Everything lies in a heap on the bed, except there's something stuck in a corner of the packet. I reach inside and pull out the little silver ring I gave Mum for her birthday. Thirty-four. She died on her thirty-fourth birthday. That morning we'd had cake and candles, and she made a wish. She didn't keep it secret, she said it out loud, she wished we could stop running.

I try the ring on my little finger, it fits. I'd like to leave it on but Gran might notice. I don't want her asking no questions.

I slip the ring back in the envelope and scoop up the other stuff. The hairbrush catches the light, gold hairs shining. I pull one out and wind it round my finger. Deep shudders shake my body, an earthquake of sadness. If I give in to it, if I let myself cry, I'll be overwhelmed. I grit my teeth and shove the hairbrush out of sight. There's just one thing lying on the bed now, the remaining starry blue slide. I snatch it up and grip it so tight it digs into my palm. I squeeze my hand and curse.

"What you doing up there?"

Quickly I shove everything into my bag and lie back

159

on the bed, folding my good arm under my head and staring at the ceiling. I'm glad I didn't throw Mum's stuff away, it's no use to me but I'm glad I've got it, glad they didn't give it to Him. Well, they couldn't, could they? They don't know where he is. I reckon the scuds could find him if they really wanted to, but I bet they haven't tried. They're not interested. Nobody's asking questions now. It's like Mum was never really here. They gave me her things and that's it, she's gone, gone in a puff of smoke. Well, I haven't forgotten and I won't let them forget. When I kill him, justice will be done and everybody will know about it. Mum's photo will be in the papers, front page news. SON KILLS FATHER IN REVENGE ATTACK. I'll make sure everybody understands what he did.

I sit up and listen. Gran's put the TV on. She's lost interest in me. I fish some felt tips out of my bag and write Mum's name in big letters on my pot arm. I draw flowers round it. Then, below it, I draw a dagger with blood dripping from the tip and I draw a heart, not a neat, symbol heart but a real one with muscles and arteries. I imagine it's his heart, imagine how I'm going to stop it beating, the blood will flow out till there's not a drop left.

In the gathering darkness, I smile. It's too dark to draw anything else so I drop the felt tips back into my bag. It's getting cold in the room so I put on my fleece. The street lights come on outside and the room gathers a yellow glow. The orange curtains turn a nasty mustard colour. It's depressing. If Gran got rid of some of the heavy pieces of dark furniture the room would look better. My eyes are drawn to the wardrobe on the opposite wall. It's big enough to hide in. Stupid idea, but it takes root – I look away but my eyes swivel back and finally, I have to get up and check it out.

The handle is an iron hoop. I twist and pull. The door sticks then flies open, throwing me backwards. I stumble against the bedframe, straighten up and switch on the light. Hesitantly, I creep forward to peer inside. A smell like mouldy bread makes my nose wrinkle. On the bottom shelf there are plastic bags, hats and a pair of silver dancing shoes, hanging above are some fusty old clothes. I pull them aside and discover, in the middle of them, a man's spanking new suit. It's modern, trendy, made of black, shiny material. This suit never belonged to Grandad. This is just the sort of sharp suit he'd wear, I'm sure it's his.

I feel in the pockets, find half a cinema ticket, a chewing gum wrapper and a screwed-up piece of paper – a supermarket bill: milk, bread, cigarettes. On top is the date. I try to work it out. My mind whirls, I can't think, then suddenly, clear as day, I see Eric holding out the match report with the date on top. Quickly I count – this bill is three days old. Gran lied to me. Two days ago, he was here.

The door creaks. I jump, but it's only Griffy wandering in. I shove the stuff back in the suit pocket and sit on the bed. I've got to think. Griffy jumps up and lies beside me. "What's going on, Griffy? What's she plotting, eh?"

"Is that dog up there? What're you doing?"

Gran's voice is loud. She'll be up in a minute. I slide the knife under the bag.

"What are we going to do?" I whisper to Griffy. "How are we going to get out of this one?"

Griffy snuffles and rubs her head on the bedspread, when she looks up her hair forms a quiff. I smoothe it down, she sighs and flops to sleep. Not for long though, there's a loud knock on the front door and she jumps up.

"Quiet, Griffy!"

I hear Gran walk through and unlock the door. A man's voice echoes up the stairs. I reach for the knife. My fingers tremble as they run down its full length. I hold the blade and turn it so the handle points down, then I lean forward and thrust it deep into my sock. The blade sticks up next to my calf so I pull a thick elastic band from my pocket, slip it over my trainer and anchor the knife to my leg. A hidden weapon.

The man's voice sounds again. My heart races as I grab Griffy's collar. Creeping out on to the landing, I slide down the top few stairs. I'm stopped in my tracks when I see who it is.

"You got here quickly," I hear Gran say.

162

"Mart was pleased to hear the news. How is he?" the man says.

"I don't know, Steve," Gran says. "I can't weigh him up."

"He always was a funny kid."

I creep back up the stairs.

"What happened to you?" I hear Gran say. "Somebody take a dislike to you?"

"Don't ask," Steve replies.

I peer over the banister and see Steve stroke his swollen face. He moves closer to Gran and speaks softly. "Look, about Davey. Don't tell him where we're going tomorrow; say I'm taking him to the cinema or something. I'll leave Martin to do the talking when he sees him."

He closes the front door and speaks softer still so that I have to risk being seen to hear him. "Mart wants the car so I'll be over about eleven tomorrow. Have the kid ready."

"All right," Gran nods, her red corkscrew curls bobbing.

"Where is he now?" Steve asks.

"Upstairs in the front bedroom." She gestures, half-turns and catches sight of me. As she lets out a sharp cry of surprise, Griffy breaks free and bounds down the stairs.

"What the . . . bloody hell." Steve staggers back against the door as Griffy jumps up at him.

"Down, get down," he yells. "Arghh, my ribs!" He moves sideways rubbing at his chest.

"You'd better come down," Gran shouts.

When I walk down she smiles as if she's pleased to see me. "Davey, you remember your Dad's mate Steve, don't you? Well, he's offered to take you to the cinema tomorrow, isn't that kind of him?"

I glare.

Steve grins. "Yeah. I heard you'd had a bit of a rough time, thought I'd give you a treat. Anything particular you'd like to see?"

I open my mouth to speak but I can't. Before they realize what I'm doing I yank the door open, push past them and run headlong up the street. Before I turn the corner I glance back and see Gran standing a few steps away from the house, hanging with all her might on to Griffy's collar. I hesitate for a split-second but I can't go back. I turn the corner and flee.

sixteen

When I finally pause for breath I'm in a street of big brick houses. I haven't got a clue where I am, don't even know how I got here, I've lost all sense of direction. I just ran and ran, looking over my shoulder, thinking any moment Gran or Steve would come racing after me in the car. Now, I'm knackered, the elastic band I put round the knife is cutting into my leg and I've got a blister on my heel.

I limp along, thinking what a complete idiot I've been. Why the hell did I run from Gran's house, after all the trouble it took me to get there? If I'd kept my cool, Steve would have taken me to see Him tomorrow, delivered me right into the enemy camp. It was a cinch – all I had to do was pretend I'd scarpered from the foster home so's I could be with Him, then wait for the right moment and *bang*! I could have done it. I'm an ace liar, had plenty of practice. One night when me and

Mum were staying in some flats I heard Him breaking in. Stupid sod never thought we had a phone. I called the scuds, told them we'd got a burglar. You should have heard me laugh when they carted him away.

I'm not feeling so clever now, though. I'm cold and hungry, my leg's going numb and I've got nowhere to sleep. I try to find some shelter sitting on a stone wall underneath a big tree. Rain drips from the branches, trickles down my forehead and runs down my neck. When I pull the collar of my fleece up, it's like a wet flannel. Things can't get much worse. My bag with all my stuff in is back at Gran's, I've got no coat and hardly any money and Griffy's a prisoner. If Griffy was with me at least we could cuddle up and keep warm. Gran had better treat her right, I hope she's given her some supper.

I cross my legs and rest my broken arm on my knee, it's aching like mad. Huddling up as best I can, I stick my good hand in my pocket and shiver. My fingers touch something – a piece of card. I pull it out and hold it up to the light. EVIE AND DENNIS THORNTON. . . Thank God I did her a good turn.

It's late by the time I'm hobbling up Kedleston Road. I've asked about a million people for directions and now at last I'm in the right street. Set back from the road are some rambling brick houses with signs outside, one is a dentist's, another is a nursery; a dog barks, lights blaze from a glass church. I check the numbers and stand outside a wide iron gate. It's a big house with a door in the middle and windows each side, the sort of house little kids draw. A light's on in one of the front windows and there's a glow from a side porch.

I walk up the path, go round to the porch and press an illuminated doorbell. After a few seconds, I hear footsteps and Evie Thornton appears at the glass door. She looks surprised to see me but when she opens the door, she smiles.

"David, isn't it? We met at the station. Come in."

I follow her into a kitchen that smells of coffee and has a palm tree growing by the sink. I start to shiver in the warmth.

"You do look wet. Stay there. I'll get you a warm towel," Evie says.

She leaves the room. It's a big kitchen, shiny tiled floor, a dresser with lots of mugs, bright paintings, a row of copper pans and plants everywhere. I stand still, aware of my muddy shoes on the clean tiles. She comes back holding out a thick warm towel and a blue sweater.

"Here. Dry yourself and put this on. I'll make you a hot drink. Would you like tea or coffee?"

"Tea, please," I say, still hovering on the tiles.

"Don't worry about the mess, take your shoes off if you want," Evie says. "I'll make the tea then we'll go through to the sitting room, there's a fire in there."

167

I rub at my stubbly head and wipe my face, unzip my wet fleece and pull it off. Luckily the jumper she's brought me is so big I can get my pot arm in it. When I pull it down it's over my knees.

Evie turns round and laughs. "My attempt at knitting," she says. "I told Dennis it would come in handy one day."

I smile but then I see her looking at my muddy shoes. I daren't take them off, not in front of her, the knife might fall out.

"Are your feet wet?" she asks.

"Er, I'll take my shoes off in a minute," I say.

Evie smiles. She's nice. She probably thinks I've got holes in my socks. I sit down and hide my feet under the table, then watch as she pours boiling water into a blue teapot. The blue teapot makes me think of Jill and when I see the blue mug on the tray my stomach turns over. It's exactly the same kind of mug that Jill uses. I press the towel against my eyes. *Don't think about Jill, she's history. You'll never go back there.*

"Do you like it sweet?"

I lower the towel and see Evie looking at me. She's asking me a question but it's like she's talking a foreign language, my brain's shut up shop. I blink, shake my head and her words filter through.

"Do you want sugar?"

I nod. "Yes, two please."

She puts the sugar bowl on the table. "Help yourself.

168

I've got a glass of wine in the other room, so I won't have one. I was just settling down to read when the doorbell rang." She waits while I spoon in two sugars, then she fires the million pound question.

"Now, what are you doing here?"

I look away, carefully drape the towel over a chair back, pat it down, give my tea another stir.

Evie's waiting. She's no pushover, I know my answer had better be good.

"My dad wasn't in," I say, cupping my hand round the warm mug.

She looks shocked. "He was expecting you, wasn't he?"

I nod. "Yeah, but he must have got mixed up, he's not very good with dates. The next-door neighbour said he's coming back tomorrow."

"Oh dear," Evie says. "That was disappointing."

"Yes," I say. "I wanted him to be there."

Evie's eyes are sharp, she's weighing everything up.

"Where did he go?"

"He went to, er . . . I'm not sure, I think he went to London."

Evie frowns. "And there's nobody you could contact, no other relatives in Derby?"

I shake my head. "I don't know nobody else in Derby. Dad came to work here when him and Mum split up." I sip my tea, playing for time. I swallow and look at Evie with my most innocent expression.

"I didn't know what to do when he wasn't in. It was freezin' outside, then I remembered you. You said I could come here whenever I wanted."

Evie's voice is full of sympathy. "I'm glad you remembered me, David. I hate to think of you spending the night on the streets." She leans forward, gently touches my hand and smiles. "Good job I was in."

She seems satisfied but the next moment her eyebrows crinkle and she looks puzzled. "What have you done with your dog?" she asks.

I have to think fast. "I. . . I . . . didn't know if you'd want her, some people don't like dogs in the house so I . . . er . . . I left her in Dad's shed." I flick my eyes downward and put on a sad expression. "I wish I hadn't now."

Evie looks worried. "Will she be safe?"

"Yeah, course. I wouldn't have left her in danger."

Evie nods. "Hmm. Well, it's too late to go gallivanting off to rescue her now. As long as she'll be all right."

"She'll be OK. She won't bark or anything."

Evie hesitates, then seems to make up her mind. "It's not the best solution but it will have to do. First thing in the morning we'll go and get her. Now, are you hungry?"

I realize I'm starving and accept an offer of beans on toast. While Evie's busy I take the opportunity to whip

170

off my shoe and inspect my leg. It's itching like mad where the elastic's been but it's not gone black or anything.

"Here you are. I've done you two slices."

As she turns round, I swiftly tuck my leg under the table.

Setting a plate down she tells me she's just going to "nip and lock the door and put the outside light off". She disappears and I hear her rattling around in the porch. Good, I think, that's me safe for the night, but when she comes back she's looking so worried I half expect Gran or Steve to rush in behind her.

"I feel we should telephone somebody, tell them you're here," she says. "It doesn't seem right. Does your dad have a mobile?"

I wish she'd stop fussing, but I mustn't get ratty or I'll blow everything, so I gently shake my head and patiently explain, "It got stolen."

"Fair enough, that's it then," she says. "We might as well settle down and relax."

She gives me such a big, warm smile that I feel shitty for lying. She's nice, much nicer than Gran, Gran's like an old witch compared to Evie. Evie's face is bright and rosy, like a bowl of tomato soup. She makes me feel comfortable and warm inside. My mouth starts to turn up at the corners, a smile grows and spreads across my face, my skin feels stiff as my cheeks crinkle. I try to grit my teeth and frown. I've got to be on my guard, don't relax, don't blow it, but I can't help wanting to impress Evie. I find myself adding bits to my story.

"I don't want to phone nobody," I say. "If I phone Auntie Sue she'll be real worried and she's had enough worry lately."

Evie nods. "You're a very thoughtful boy," she says. "Well, I suppose it can't do any harm for one night."

I could have left it there but the thing is, once you start telling lies you can't stop. "Auntie Sue thinks I'm with Dad and Dad thinks I'm with Auntie Sue," I say. "It's much easier if they don't know."

"I understand," Evie says.

I'm glad she does cos I'm beginning to believe it myself. "They've had a lot of worry with Mum dying," I say.

"Of course they have and so have you, you poor thing," Evie says. She gives my shoulder a squeeze and makes a sympathetic clicking noise with her tongue. I almost tell her more but just in time I stop myself. "Liars need good memories," Mum used to say.

"Would you like some cake or biscuits?" Evie asks.

"No," I say. I scoop up the last of the beans, they turn to dry mush in my mouth. I don't want anything else to eat. Mum used to make me beans on toast, Mum used to cut the bread into soldiers.

I follow Evie down a corridor into a big, bright room. The carpet's blue and the walls glow golden yellow in the firelight.

"Sit down," Evie says, pointing to a big red sofa.

I carefully hide one leg behind the other as I sink into the big red cushions. It's warm in this room and I feel safe. I'd like to stay here, stay and forget about everything that's happened, pretend I'm Evie's grandson and I'm on a long holiday. My mum and dad are rich, they're in a foreign country and some time they'll come for me, but not yet. My head lolls back, I slide sideways and come to with a jolt. Don't start going soft. You can't afford to relax. *You've got a bloody knife stuck down your sock. How're you going to explain that if she sees it?* I stiffen my shoulders and sit up straight.

"Warmer now?" Evie asks.

I nod.

"I'll just put a bit more coal on, it'll soon burn up."

Keeping an eye on Evie while she kneels in front of the fire, I roll up my trouser leg, grab the knife and stuff it behind a cushion. I'm just patting the cushion back into place when Evie turns round. My heart thumps and blood rushes to my face. I lean on the cushion.

"Oh, I've not stoked the fire up too much, have I?" Evie says. "You look hot."

I don't answer. I'm too busy trying to breathe normally.

"Are you all right?" she asks.

I feel my face getting redder so to avoid her gaze I bend down and roll the elastic band off my leg. I do it

173

without thinking and suddenly, I stop. She'll think I'm up to something, that I'm doing something weird, she'll start asking questions. I bite my lip. *For God's sake, You've hidden the knife, it's only an elastic band.*

Evie chuckles "Were you trying to remember something?" she asks.

"No. . . I . . . er. . ." I say, feeling relieved. "I was trying to keep my legs dry."

Evie grins. "That was a habit of Dennis's," she says. "Always secured his trousers with elastic bands when we were hiking."

She brushes her hands together, then sits down in a big chair opposite me. Leaning forward, she picks up a glass of wine and sips. "I've got a bed made up so it's no problem to have you stay," she says. She tucks her legs underneath her and takes another drink of wine. "Well, this is an unexpected pleasure, to have some young company. Now what shall we do till bedtime? Would you like to play a game? I've got a chest full of board games my grandchildren like to raid when they visit."

I try to look interested but all I want to do is sleep, my eyes are almost closing as the heat from the fire seeps into me.

"Another time, perhaps," Evie says. "We'll watch a bit of telly and then bed."

She finds the remote and flicks the telly on. A hospital programme finishes and is followed by the news. A posh woman in a suit tells us there's been a suicide bombing in the Middle East. They show pictures of women wailing, tears streaming down their faces. The mother of the bomber isn't crying, she looks proud and happy.

"I don't understand what motivates a young girl to kill herself like that," Evie says.

I know, but I don't say nothing – it's simple – revenge! The rest of the news is no better; murder, thieving, corrupt politicians. It's all horrible. I lean back, close my eyes and try to think of something good. Eventually I settle on the day me and Mum got the house in Chesterfield. We were happy, it was a new start and the first time we'd got a proper place of our own after two years of flitting about hiding in grotty flats or other people's houses or the shelter. Miss Social Worker told us we'd be safe in our new house, that he wouldn't find us, and we believed her. Mum talked about buying paint and making curtains, her eyes were shining, not scared any more. That was three weeks before she died. Three weeks, that's all it took Him.

I jolt awake and look across at Evie. She's dozing. The telly's playing to itself. On the screen another woman with big earrings is saying something about the scuds doing a double search for a missing boy and his father, concentrating on the Derby area. My breath catches in my throat. There's a photo of me on the screen. It's an old one, my hair's long. I've changed a lot and now I've got a scar on my forehead, but if you looked close, you'd know it was me. I glance at Evie, her eyes are still shut. I gasp as a phone number appears on the screen.

"Police want to interview Martin Dawson, the boy's father who is believed to be living in the Derby area." A mugshot of Him in his Derby scarf flashes up.

"Who's that?" Evie asks, leaning forward.

I gulp. "Oh . . . erm . . . a bank robber," I say.

My heart's racing. My eyes flick from the screen to Evie. I wonder just how much she's seen and heard. Thankfully, she doesn't look alarmed, just slightly puzzled. She blinks and gets up. "I'll go and put a hot-water bottle in your bed. You need some sleep and so do I, we're both tired."

As soon as she leaves, I pull the knife from its hiding place and shove it under the cushion I'm sitting on. As long as Evie doesn't hear the news tonight, I should be safe. In the morning, I'll have to be up early, get the knife and scarper before she wakes. I can pull it off as long as I don't arouse her suspicions. No more blushing or stumbling over words.

To calm myself down I get up and wander round the room, looking at the big, bold paintings on the walls. I'm not sure what they're meant to be but I like the colours. One is all earthy browns, yellows and oranges but it's not dull, it's really alive. In the corner of each painting there's the initials, E T. At first, I think of an alien but then it dawns on me that they're Evie's initials. She must be a painter.

In a basket next to the armchair I spot a sketch pad and a box of charcoals. Leafing through the drawings, I see lots of stone walls, hills and cliff edges. I nearly drop the book when Evie comes into the room.

"It's all right," she says. "I don't mind you looking."

"They're good," I say. "I like the shapes. Did you do them all?"

Evie smiles. "Yes."

"I like drawing," I say. I hadn't meant to say it. I don't usually tell nobody, not straight off anyway because they can make fun of you. Evie's not that type though, she thinks about what you say, takes it serious.

"I'd like to see some of your drawings," she says.

I don't answer because I'm thinking about where they are, back in my room at Jill's. Fat chance of me ever seeing them again.

It doesn't matter that I don't answer because Evie's off on a memory trip of her own. "I took up painting when I retired," she says. "We spent some lovely days up on the edges, Dennis and I." She goes over to a shiny table and picks up a photo. "We'd take a picnic and Dennis would go off for a walk or sit and read while I sat sketching." She holds out a photo in a big silver frame. "This was taken at one of our favourite places, Robin Hood's Stride."

The man with his arm round Evie is tall and thin with silver hair.

"How did Dennis die?" I ask.

Evie looks surprised and hesitates for a moment. Then she says, "He had a heart attack."

"Were you with him?" I ask.

"Yes, I was," she says.

"Were you glad you were there?" I ask.

"Yes," she says. "I was glad."

I look at her and want to cry.

"Were you with your mum?" she asks.

"Yes, but I wasn't no use. I didn't do nothing to help her. He pushed her down the stairs. She hit her head. He killed her."

Evie stares at me. "Oh, my good Lord," she says.

seventeen

As the town wakes up, I'm running from Evie's house, back to Pilot Street. Every nerve is throbbing, tension zinging through me like live wire. I know I haven't got much time, the list of people looking for me is growing longer. That's not going to stop me though. I dreamt about Mum last night, the same dream I always have. She's falling in slow-motion, her arms spread out, hair streaming like gold ribbon, she shouts, I try to catch her but she slips through my arms. When I woke my stomach felt heavy as cement and my face was wet with tears. I don't care how many people are looking for me, somehow I'll get Him.

There's not much traffic or folks about at this hour. I'm proud of myself for waking up so early and slipping out of Evie's house without her hearing me and I'm all prepared, got the knife secured to my leg. I'm becoming real good at this criminal stuff, I could be a burglar if I wanted. And I'm a genius remembering my way back to Gran's. It's not light yet but I have no problem retracing my steps, it's like a map in my brain – go down to the roundabout, cross the road, turn right, past the cathedral, through to where the big shops are and up to the hospital.

All the time I'm walking I keep a lookout for scuds, clocking hiding places just in case I have to dodge into one. I've given up running because I don't want to attract attention but I'm not dawdling either; the sooner I get to Gran's the better. I can't see no scuds about yet, but with me being on the run, they'll have my description. For that matter anybody could suss me, any ruddy clever Dick that remembers me from the telly last night.

Anyway, Evie will phone the scuds, I know she will. As soon as she gets up and sees I've gone, she'll phone them. Think about it – a boy she hardly knows turns up on her doorstep, gives her some bullshit story about his dad being away and he's left his dog in a shed. Then he says he's got nowhere to stay the night and oh, by the way, his dad killed his mum. The next morning, the boy does a runner. . . She's bound to call the scuds. I suppose that's my fault, I was an idiot to tell her about Him, but I'm not sorry. If anything happens to me, somebody will know the truth.

As I pass the hospital I see lights come on, people waking up with broken legs and bandages. Mum was in there once, the DRI it's called. I remember going to see her. He took me, we bought some flowers, I chose them, they were yellow. We had some food in a cafe. I can't remember nothing else. Anyway, I don't want to remember, cos that day he was all right, he was nice, like he could be sometimes. I stop and look through some gates, see ambulances waiting. I breathe through my nose, deep snorting gasps. *You idiot, you great soft wally. Don't forget what he did, don't ever think there's any good in Him. He probably put Mum in that hospital, that's probably why he was being nice. He's scum, a monster, a raving maniac and he deserves to die.*

I grit my teeth and set off to cover the last few streets, I picture his face, remember how his mouth would tighten, the muscle in his cheek twitch, his fist clench and he'd let fly. He couldn't control his temper. Mum lived in fear, never knowing what would spark him off – it was like living with a volcano.

When I reach the school at the bottom of Gran's street it's getting light. A watery sun is breaking through but it's still cold and my breath makes smoky circles in the air. I stop and lean against the school railings. I wonder if Griffy's awake, wonder if she senses I'm close. There's nobody about yet, nobody walking to work, no kids in the school playground, a couple of cars go past but that's all. Across the street I see his hideous red car parked by the kerb in front of Gran's house. All I've got to do is get inside and Steve will take me to Him. *This is it, this is the test.*

I cross the road and take a quick recce up and down Gran's street. There's no place to hide but I'm due some good luck and it's dustbin day, wheelie bins line the pavement. Opposite Gran's, I dodge behind one and crouch down. With relief I notice Gran's front curtains are still drawn. I wish I could rescue Griffy but I can't, I mustn't even think about it, I've got to be cool, super-cool, as sly and cunning as Him. Anyway, Griffy's not yelping or anything, if she was in trouble I'd hear her and Gran's not that bad, she must like dogs because she gave Griffy a bone. *Don't think about Griffy. Keep your mind on the job, no distractions.*

I take another swift shufti up and down the street then run across to the car and pull at the driver's door. Just as I suspected, it's locked. Well, it was worth a try. I lean against the window pushing against it with my back. There's no movement. I push again. You'd think the windows on an old banger like this would move. I rub my back up and down and there's a slight rattle.

A man comes out of a house, it's the man I saw yesterday pulling a little dog. He glances at me, I bend down as if I'm looking for something. He wanders on, down the street. When he's gone I find a fifty-pence piece in my pocket and try pushing it between the glass and the rim. I manage to force a slight opening but can't widen it. Damn. I'm not sure what to do now, maybe I could try the other window but I'm aware that any moment, Gran might open her curtains and catch me.

Another door behind me rattles, and a bunch of people come out. A girl in a long dress stands and stares, her huge dark eyes gazing intently from under a white scarf. I look away, lean my back against the car window and hope she'll think I'm waiting for someone. Her mother takes hold of her hand and murmurs something, pulling her away. As they walk off, the girl turns round. My mouth dries, my heart quickens, I'm sure she's on to me. I imagine her shouting, "That's the boy they're looking for! He was on the news."

I'm so busy watching the girl that I don't see the scud car. It's almost on me before I realize. I see a flash of white and orange, blue letters and eyes staring into a mirror. They've clocked me. How could they miss? I'm leaning on his car, I might as well have a big WANTED poster on my head. Any moment now, the car will stop, the doors fly open and I'll be arrested. I daren't move, I hardly dare breathe. *Easy, easy, keep calm.* Centimetre by centimetre, I slide my feet sideways, moving towards the back of the car. I duck down behind the boot. A pulse throbs in my ears, my heart beats like it has giant wings. I've no chance. But to my amazement, I hear the car drive off. I wait a moment, check and let out a long sigh of relief. They must be complete idiots, they've missed me – my luck is holding.

I know it's only a matter of time though, if I don't

disappear I'm bound to be discovered. Without much hope I press the button that opens the boot. Bingo! The lid springs up. It's empty except for a few old rags and a rusty spanner. I make a quick decision, it's risky but it's my best chance. I jump inside and pull down the lid; the catch clicks shut.

It's dark and stuffy, I haven't got much room to move and there are big questions in my head. Will I suffocate? Will I ever be able to get out? I hear voices, a car engine starts up, a dog barks, I think it's Griffy. If it is she might sniff me out. I wait and wait trying not to move, trying to control my breathing, trying not to panic. After a while my legs are so cramped they hurt. I almost think of giving up and forcing my way back out, but after what seems an age I feel the car jolt, a door bangs, the engine starts up – I'm moving.

It's torture. As the car swings round corners my head bumps and judders. Exhaust fumes seep in and make me feel sick and it's getting hotter. I clamp my hand over my mouth and roll to a place where I can breathe more easily. It's better, but I'm still boiling, sweaty and thirsty.

The car slows down, stops, then jumps forward lurching to the left. My head hits something hard. I think we're circling a big roundabout. We speed up and seem to be on a fast road, I can hear other traffic. For a while it's a bit easier as the car drives straight but then we turn off the main road and I lose concentration as

I'm jolted backwards and forwards. It's like a bad fairground ride and pain's jabbing through my broken arm.

We twist and bump along rough ground, I hear gravel scrunch and ping against metal, I smell burning rubber. The car shudders over a grid and I bash my head on the boot. Just when I think I can't stand any more and I'll have to hammer to get out, we stop.

The engine is switched off, the car door opens. Footsteps crunch on the gravel, there's a faint knock on a distant door, muffled voices, a door closes.

I push at the boot lid but it's firmly shut. I fumble around feeling for the spanner, find it and squirm round so I can push at the catch. It doesn't move. I hear footsteps, a girl is singing.

I've got to get out somehow. If I don't, I'll end up in his hands. I bang the spanner on the boot lid. The singing stops. I knock again. I hear the lock being pressed and the lid springs open. A girl about my age looks down at me with wide eyes.

"What the hell are you doing in there?" she demands.

"I got stuck," I say.

She laughs. "You want to be careful."

I sit up, look around and see I'm on a caravan site.

"Do you live here?" I ask.

"Yeah, sometimes," she says.

"Where is it?" I ask.

"Derwent," she tells me.

I clamber over the rim of the boot and start to move towards some bushes. She follows me. "What's going off?" she asks. "Why were you really in there?" I dodge behind the bushes. "You in trouble?"

"Did you see where the man driving the car went?" I ask.

"Yeah," she says and points to a long green caravan. "He went into that one."

"Do you know who lives there?"

"It's a woman with a baby and a man's there sometimes."

"What does the man look like?"

"Tall, brown wavy hair, not bad looking for an oldish bloke."

It sounds like Him but I never reckoned on Him having company.

"Right, thanks," I say.

"Why do you want to know?" the girl asks.

"I'm looking for my dad," I tell her.

"Oh," she says. She looks over at the caravan and frowns. "You're the second person who's asked about that caravan today."

"Who else was asking?"

"Tall woman in a grey suit, bright blue eyes, blonde hair in a ponytail."

A shiver of alarm goes through me. "Was she in a police car?" I ask.

"Didn't see," the girl says.

Her eyes narrow and I sense she's going to tell me more but at that moment a voice calls loudly, "Alice. . . Alice."

"That's me," the girl says. "I'd better go. We're off canoeing. Good luck."

She runs over to a white van and climbs inside. I watch from the bushes as it drives off, then I edge my way round to the green caravan.

Woods slope down to the back window, there's washing on the line, stained tea towels and a woman's knickers. I hadn't thought about Him shacking up with somebody else. Bastard, why did he come looking for Mum if he's living with another woman?

I move to the window and try to look through but I'm not tall enough. The door opens, I hear voices. I creep round to the side. Steve comes down the front steps followed by a woman, she's wearing a white shirt and black jeans, her hair's a reddish colour and piled up on top of her head.

"I'll come straight back," she calls to somebody inside the caravan.

I watch Steve and the woman go over to the car and get in. The woman is driving; gravel crunches as she turns the wheel and heads off.

Now it's time. I reach down, roll up my trouser leg and pull out the knife. I stroke the sharp blade. I don't feel nervous any more, I just want it to happen. I want it to be over, I want to watch Him die. He'll see me standing over him and before he loses consciousness, he'll know I've done it. I pull out the knife and draw it across my pot arm, cutting into the plaster. *This is for you, Mum, this is for you.*

I walk slowly along the side of the caravan and up the steps. I feel calm as I reach for the handle. Nothing's going to stop me. Gently, I open the door.

It's dim inside and my eyes have to get used to it. There's a wall facing me and an open space to my left. As I turn and walk into the room I hold the knife out in front of me. He's sitting watching TV and he's cradling a baby.

"Davey?"

He looks up at me. Light flashes on the knife.

"What the hell are you doing here?" he asks urgently.

"What does it look like?" I snap.

My hand tightens on the knife handle.

"Put the baby down," I say.

"Don't be silly," he laughs.

"Put it down," I say.

He stares at me, his mouth open. "You're not joking, right?" His lip curls. "You little bastard."

I step forward and point the knife at his throat. His eyes widen. "All right, I'll put her down."

He's scared. His hands tremble as he puts the baby on the couch beside him. I shove the knife in front of his eyes, one move and I'll puncture his eyeball.

"Move and you're dead," I say.

188

My voice sounds loud and confident but I'm struggling to stop it shaking. He looks up. There's a gap at his throat, a gap where the knife could slide in. I try to keep my hand steady.

He starts to plead with me, his voice quivering. "This is about your mum, right? Don't, Davey. I didn't mean it to happen. I've been beside myself. I loved her."

By his side the baby kicks and gurgles. Anger wells up inside me. "How can you say you loved her when you were living here with somebody else? You've even got a baby!" I yell.

He reaches for my hand but I jab the knife down and He cowers back against the wall.

"I did love her. This was only temporary. I always knew I'd come back – me and Ali, we'd be together."

"You killed her, you killed her on her birthday," I say.

His mouth twists, his face crumples. "I never meant to kill her, Davey. I just wanted to see her." His words come out all mangled like he's choking but I don't let it bother me.

"You're lying," I say. "You were always hurting her."

"No, Davey, you've got it all wrong."

Suddenly his hand darts forward trying to knock the knife away but I'm too quick. He bends over moaning, a thin streak of blood running from his knuckles.

"You swine, you little sod. You're bloody crazy. It was an accident, an accident. She fell down the bloody stairs."

"You pushed her," I shout.

His shoulders tense and I think that any minute he's going to jump me. I'm no match for him even with the knife so I've got to do it now. Stab him, deep and hard. My hand closes on the handle. I lift my arm but just as I'm going to thrust the knife down, the baby starts to cry.

He leans over, protecting it, shushing and blubbering. His hand is dripping blood, deep sobs shake his whole body. I hate him, I hate the stupid, useless, pathetic sod. I aim a kick at his shin, *smash*. He picks the baby up and cowers against the wall. I kick him again and again, smash into his legs. He blubs and pulls his legs up on to the couch, still rocking and crying.

"Murderer," I shout. "Murderer!"

He swivels round. "No, Davey, no."

I kick at his knee and he cries out.

"I loved her, I always loved her."

"You killed her."

I grip the knife tight and this time I thrust it down, stab, stab. I twist it round, pull it out and stab again and again.

There's a shout, then lots of voices, the baby's wailing and I'm shoved to the floor. Someone's holding me down. I taste blood in my mouth.

"Come on, Davey, it's all over."

I squirm sideways and see a strand of blonde hair. No escape. Sergeant Gardner's got me pinned to the floor.

190

eighteen

David, where did the knife come from?

I close my eyes and hum a tune inside my head. Hum, hum, hum, dee, dum. Mum used to say, "music feeds the soul". I didn't understand that but I know music made her happy. She listened to everything, all sorts, even stuff with no words, she'd fiddle with the radio till she found something she liked. "Don't close your mind to any sort of music," she'd say, but I enjoyed it best when she danced to Radio One. Hum, hum, hum, dee, dum. "Dancin' in the Street", she loved that one. She was happy when she was dancing.

Who did the knife belong to, David?

I can hear a clock ticking, a telephone ringing. Tick, tock, silent moments sliding by. I scan the room for the clock but can't see it. I try to remember the words to the song in my head.

How did you get to the caravan?

It's the Inspector bloke asking questions. Inspector Colin Burden. We're in a room at the scud station and he's sitting opposite me. The room's hot and stuffy and smells of disinfectant. Sergeant Gardner's here too, looking anxious, willing me to answer questions, back to our old routine. On my side of the table there's Miss SW Sarah and a woman solicitor – a cosy little group.

The Inspector's mouth is flapping. He's either repeating his question, or it's an echo I'm hearing, caravan, caravan. Dum, de, dum, dum de dum. I'm trying hard not to listen but his voice filters through.

Can you tell us why you ran away from your foster home?

Course I can. Does he think I'm stupid or what? I can tell him every detail but I'm not going to. I squint at him. He looks like an idiot, his head is bald but he's combed long hairs over his shiny scalp to try and fool people.

I slump down in my chair and focus on my hands. They're both the same size now. The hand with the pot was much bigger before, swollen up like a baseball mitt, but now it's normal – probably the only thing about me that is. My vision blurs, my eyes water. I don't think they should be asking me questions, I'm in no fit state. I was shaking in the scud car, Louise said it was delayed shock, she gave me a drink of sweet tea. I felt a bit better after that but then they started grilling me.

I'm not saying anything. I don't want to talk. I don't

want to think. I wish my mind was just one big blank. I wish I were dead.

Pictures flash and freeze like a video behind my eyelids. His car, red as blood, the car boot dark as a dungeon, Him in the caravan, gob wide open, eyes starin'. I gave him a fright – he was scared to death when he saw that knife.

Did you take a knife to the caravan, David? Was it your knife?

I stabbed him, rammed the knife in as far as I could, sliced down, pulled it out, thrust it in again and again. It was brilliant, a rush of pure excitement, surging and thundering like a giant wave. Crash! Pow!

When Louise threw herself at me, I didn't care, my job was done. The scuds could do what they liked to me, I was filled with triumph. He could go to hell where he belonged. I was grinning like a mad donkey as Louise pulled me to my feet but she didn't grin back, she looked serious, her mouth set tight.

"David, are you all right?" she asked.

Course I'm all right, I thought, shouldn't you be worried about ape man bleeding to death on the floor? Perrins wasn't bothered either, he wasn't administering first aid or phoning for an ambulance, he was just standing staring at me, puffing out his cheeks and blowing a long stream of air up over his face. "Phew," he said, "That. . ."

The rest of what he said was drowned out by a loud

wail, a strange sort of animal noise issuing from behind him. He turned round, and as he moved, I saw Him. He wasn't writhing on the floor, he wasn't dead or anywhere near it – he was on the seat, face pale as putty, nursing his cut hand. There was no blood gushing from his chest, no big red stain splashed across his white T-shirt, he was just sitting there, trembling and blubbing.

I couldn't take it in, I just stared and stared. Nobody moved or said anything until the baby started to kick its legs and howl. Sobbing, he dived to pick it up, cradling it to his chest, his tears splashing all over its face. I hated him more than ever then, hated him holding that baby like he loved it.

Perrins said something to him, I don't know what, I can't remember. I was too shocked, all the triumph drained out of me. I thought I'd killed him but I hadn't, I hadn't even really hurt him. It was then I started trembling. If Louise hadn't been holding my arm I would have collapsed, but she was holding me tight and I had to watch him muttering to the baby, rocking it back and forth until Perrins took it from him and another scud led him outside.

"Come on, David," Louise said to me. "It's all over."

Just before I turned away, another scud came forward, bent down and pulled the knife out of the foam cushions. If Gardner hadn't been holding me, I would have seized that knife and stabbed myself. I'm a gutless, spineless prat. All the planning, all those big ideas, thinking I was hard. Mr Tough Guy, not talking to nobody, storing up all my anger to get back at Him. But when I had my chance, I didn't take it. I'd stabbed the ruddy cushions. He'd say it for me – "you useless little sod, you've got no balls."

Did your father take you to the caravan, David?

I ignore his question but it starts me wondering. I sit up and look at Sergeant Gardner, she's anxiously chewing on her thumbnail. Her hand drops, she sighs.

"Did your father hurt you, David?" she asks, her voice soft.

My mind starts working, I replay the scene. They rushed in, Sergeant Gardner threw herself on top of me, Perrins jumped over us to grab Him. Afterwards, they didn't shout at me or treat me like a criminal, they asked me if I was all right like they were worried about me. Of course, they didn't see what really happened – all they saw was me with the knife but I could have grabbed it from Him, I could have been trying to protect myself. *Think, David, think. If you're clever and you play this right, you can still win.*

When they took me outside there were loads of patrol cars, scuds all over the place, people watching. I saw them bundling him into a car. I bet they've brought him here. He was the one they wanted and now they've got him. He might be here, in the next room and if he is, I know he'll be telling them a pack of lies. *Be clever, be cunning. Don't let him get away with it.*

I stare at the graffiti covering the table – rude words, cartoons, people's names. I look at the drawing of the heart and dagger on my pot arm, there's a smudge of blood across it. I wish it was soaked, soaked in his blood.

What did your father say to you, David?

The Inspector's tapping his pen. I squeeze my eyes tight to concentrate, trying to think what to answer, but it's tough because I'm so tired. I've got to remember what I tell them or they'll catch me out. There's so much stuff clogging my head already and I start wondering about things that aren't important, like who's looking after the baby? Its mother would have had a shock when she returned home. She shouldn't worry though, she ought to think herself lucky, it wouldn't be long before he started beating her up. I feel sorry for the baby – they told me it's a girl. She's got a right bastard for a father. Still, if I can make one last effort, she might never know him.

Miss SW's talking. "David, Inspector Burden wants you to tell him what happened at the caravan. All you have to do is tell the truth."

My head swirls, people's faces loom like ghosts. I struggle to remember. I didn't kill him. I failed. I know that's true, but everything else starts to blur. I'm not up to this, I've been through too much. Sarah's words clang like a bell in my ears, "the truth, the truth, the truth". I remember some words from a telly programme, "the truth is out there". It was on every week, always the same plot – somebody knew something important but nobody would believe them – a bit like me. But, no, that's not true. I've never told them, I've never given them a chance to believe me. I open my eyes and look at their faces. Burden has a pen poised and on the table in front of Gardner is a tape machine. They're waiting for my evidence, my truth. Well, here it is, they're gonna get it.

I look down, squeeze my eyes together and real tears well up. I raise my head, look at Louise and gulp. "He wanted to kill me," I say. "He killed Mum and then he wanted to kill me."

Louise's expression doesn't change but I hear her breath come out as a sharp pop.

Sarah pats my shoulder. "Take your time, David," she says. "Nobody's going to hurry you. Tell us what happened and I promise you, you'll feel better."

Concentrate, David – think! This is your last chance. Nobody knows what happened at the house the day your mum died. There were no witnesses. It's your word against his.

I've got to be sharp because I know he's a good liar. He'll say he didn't mean to hurt Mum, he loved her, he'll say I'm the vicious one, I was the one with the knife, I was the one trying to stab him. He can play the innocent real good, I've seen him. He'll try and get their sympathy, say he was upset that Mum died. But, I have a sudden zinging thought, there's one major flaw in his argument – if he cared so much about her, why did he run away?

Stay calm, don't blow it. But I need time to work things out, if I make a mistake I've had it. I give a dry sob and sniff. Sarah hands me a tissue. While I wipe my face, I'm thinking hard.

"Perhaps we should leave this until tomorrow," the solicitor says. "David's obviously upset."

I blow my nose. "It's all right," I say. "I want to answer the questions, I want to help."

Louise leans forward. "Are you sure you're up to this, David?"

"Yes," I say weakly.

She smiles encouragingly. "Take some deep breaths," she says. "Don't rush it. We'll do this bit by bit, if at any time you're not comfortable, tell us and we'll stop."

She informs me she's going to record what I say which scares me a bit cos I know I'll have to be doubly careful. When she switches the tape on there's a faint buzzing, everybody seems to be holding their breath and waiting, then Louise states the time and place and who's present. I bite my lip and swallow. This is it.

Inspector Burden clears his throat. "Who took you to the caravan, David?" he asks.

That's an easy one. "His friend, Steve, took me in the boot of his car."

198

"Why did he put you in the boot?"

"He shoved me in, he didn't want nobody to see me."

"How did you meet Steve?"

This one's tricky. A lot of ideas go round in my head. "Steve phoned Jill and Eric's house. He said he'd got something of Mum's he wanted to give me so I met him but he didn't give me nothing. He just grabbed me and before I could do anythin' he shoved me into the car boot."

"And what happened then?"

"It was horrible. He was driving for ages. I thought I'd suffocate. Then when he stopped, he shoved me into the caravan and drove off. Dad was in the caravan, he said I was his prisoner, he said I had to tell the police Mum died cos of an accident – if I didn't, he'd kill me."

The Inspector's face is a mask; his expression doesn't change. His eyes are muddy brown and I can't read them, I don't know if he believes me or not. I give a dry sob and try and squeeze out a few more tears. I glance at Louise to see if she looks sympathetic but she's fiddling with the tape machine.

"I'm tired," I say. "I can't think no more."

"He should have a break," the solicitor says.

"Just a couple more questions then we can finish," Inspector Burden says. He leans forward. "On your mum's birthday, did your dad come to the house?"

I'm aware of the Inspector watching me. I blink and

swallow. "Yes," I say. "He thumped and banged till he broke the door down."

Burden writes something down, then I see him draw a big question mark. Panic surges through me. I've got to convince him. Before he can ask any more questions, I start talking.

"It was mum's birthday, he smashed his way in, pretended he'd missed us. He brought her some flowers but as soon as he was inside he started yelling and hitting her. He was angry because we'd run away from him. He said it took him a long time to find us. He dragged Mum upstairs, he shouted that if he couldn't have her then nobody could. He slammed me against the wall, then he broke my arm so I couldn't do nothing to stop him and he pushed Mum down the stairs. He did it deliberate, he wanted to kill her. It wasn't an accident. If it was an accident, he'd have stayed to help us."

When I pause for breath, Louise looks up and her eyes are full of sympathy. I can tell everything makes sense to her and that encourages me to keep going. The solicitor woman tries to interrupt but I don't let her, I start talking again and this time I tell them about things in the past, the stuff in Derby, how he made Mum lose the baby, about him dragging me out of bed at the shelter. I don't stop talking till I've done and then I start to cry. They're real tears. Talking about the past makes me upset and on top of that I'm exhausted. I can't say nothing else. It's up to them now, they've got the evidence. They can nail him.

The Inspector finishes writing and looks up. "One last question, David. Where did the knife come from?"

"I don't know," I say. "It was his."

There's a throbbing inside my head, it's pulsing and swelling with every beat until I feel it will burst. I put my hand to my forehead, lean back and cry. Louise hands me the box of tissues.

"Go on, don't worry, let it all out," she says. "You've been through a lot in the past twenty-four hours."

The Inspector and Sarah get up, turn their backs to the table and whisper. I wipe my eyes and look up at a high window with bars across it, the paint's chipped. I hope he goes somewhere with bars and they never let him out.

Sarah turns round. "You've been very brave, David," she says.

I hope they'll let me go now. I haven't done nothing wrong. I've cooperated, told them what they wanted to know. I want to go somewhere quiet now. I wish I could curl up with Griffy and go to sleep.

Sarah comes to stand beside me. I look up at her. "Have you found Griffy?" I ask.

She smiles. "We know where she is. Jill and Eric are on their way to get her, right now." She looks across at Inspector Burden and raises her eyebrows.

He nods. "Yes, we've finished. This lad's been

through a lot, he needs some rest." He picks up his notebook and pen. "You've been very cooperative, David. Well done."

As he goes out of the room, the solicitor woman picks up her briefcase. "That was quite some story," she says to Louise.

I want to hit her. "It's not a story," I shout. "It's the truth."

Louise looks concerned. "She didn't mean it like that, David. She just meant you've had a difficult time."

"Exactly," the solicitor says. She turns to Sarah. "Now, I'll need to talk to David alone. Where are you taking him?"

"I can only think of one place," Sarah says. "I'll see if I can fix it."

nineteen

I sit on my bed and open the brown envelope. Everything's here, the red purse, the blue slide, the silver ring. I had a horrible feeling that Gran would have kept something just out of spite, but she hasn't. I'm glad about that and Sarah's rescued some photos, too. I spread them out. There's Mum when she was about my age, perhaps a bit older, she's with two friends, they're all in school uniform, neat hair, ties with big knots, grinning at the camera. She didn't know how her life was going to turn out then. You have to be careful who you trust.

Sarah suggested I make a special place for Mum's things, a place where I can put a photo – she's going to buy me a frame for my favourite one. It's a good idea because I can't picture Mum's face clear enough sometimes. I try and it won't come, it really upsets me.

There's a knock on the door and Jill comes into the

room. She sits down and says she wants to talk to me. I hope it's not about me being sent away. I was lucky to come back here. I'm on trial to see if I can behave and not run away. It was Sarah who fixed it for me, she's all right, Sarah.

"That's lovely," Jill says, looking at the photo. "Your mum was beautiful."

"Yeah," I say. "But, it didn't do her no good."

Jill frowns. "David," she says, "you've got to try and. . ."

"Try and what?" I ask.

"Never mind," Jill says. "We'll talk about it later."

She looks so serious I get worried. "What's up?" I ask. "Have I got to go?"

A puzzled look crosses her face and then she gasps. "Go? Oh, good heavens, no. Of course not, you're not going anywhere."

I pick up Mum's hair slide and hold it in the palm of my hand, watching the star shine. "But, what if he isn't convicted? He could say he wants me to live with him, just to be mean."

Jill thinks for a moment, pursing her lips. "I can't promise anything, David," she says. "But with the evidence you gave, I think it unlikely your father would be granted custody of you. Anyway, you're old enough to have a big say in where you want to live."

That's a relief. I lean over and stroke Griffy. "Good," I say firmly. "Because I want to stay here."

She smiles. "I was hoping that's what you'd say." She stops smiling and looks more serious. "Now, I've got a suggestion for you. "

I'm still a bit suspicious and watch her carefully as I ask what it is.

The muscles in Jill's face seem to tighten as if she's steeling herself for something and her words come out like she's rehearsed them. "Well, I was wondering if you'd like to move into Charlotte's room?"

She doesn't say it all of a piece, she hesitates in the middle and I can tell she's thought about this a lot. I'm gobsmacked, everything in Charlotte's room's just as she left it, I thought that was how Jill wanted it. I look down at Mum's stuff, then back at Jill, and there's tears glistening in her eyes.

"It makes sense, really," she says. "It's a much bigger, brighter room and. . ." she pauses, "it'd make you really part of the family. This room was only ever meant to be temporary."

I don't know what to say and then what I do say is clumsy. "What about all her stuff?" I ask.

Jill shakes her head. "I've got to sort it out some time," she says. "Charlotte's things can't be there for ever . . . like a museum. And it's not like I need them to remember her, Charlie's here." She puts a hand over her heart and her other hand reaches out to me. She holds my hand and I don't pull away. "Life has to go on," she says.

I squeeze Jill's hand and then I say quietly, "It's only stuff."

Jill nods. "Yeah, it's only stuff."

We both sit in silence for a minute, thinking. I lean my head on Jill's shoulder and she sighs. Then suddenly, she pats my head and straightens up. "Right. If you're agreed, we'll do it, clear the room and choose some new paint and furnishings. Simon's coming next weekend, so it'll be good to get it finished before he's back."

I look down, biting my lip.

"What's wrong?" Jill asks.

I can't say anything, I'm swamped by nerves, my stomach churning.

Jill looks alarmed. "You don't have to do it, not if you don't want," she says. "I haven't pushed you into it, have I?"

"Simon," I say. "He might not like it."

Jill pats my hand. "Actually, it was Simon who suggested it."

'But it's OK with you?" I ask.

"Yes, it's OK. It will be one of the toughest things I've ever had to do, but it's time to move on."

I drop a fluffy leopard on top of the hockey boots inside the black plastic sack. Jill picks up a guitar and a bag of clothes.

"That's about everything now," she says in a brittle

voice. She doesn't move but stands looking into the distance, her arms cradling the bag. I see the muscles in her jaw twitch, her mouth sets into a hard line. For a few seconds she's still as a post, then she blinks and shakes her head.

"Nearly done," she murmurs.

I turn away, pick up the black sack and head out on to the landing.

Jill comes after me. "Thanks for helping," she says. "I couldn't have done this without you."

We bump down the stairs into the hall and out on to the drive. Jill unlocks the car boot and hoists stuff into it. I swing my bag up beside hers.

She makes a noise that's halfway between a sob and a laugh. "Charlotte would say stop being so soft, get rid of it. What's the use keeping things when other people can use them? She was very practical." She sniffs and closes the boot lid. "That's about it now."

Eric comes out of the garage and puts his arm around her. "You're sure you've saved everything you want?" he asks.

"Yes, I'm sure," Jill answers.

Eric hugs her and kisses the top of her head. I turn away and stare hard at some purple flowers. Everything's in flower now, the garden's full of colour.

Jill touches my shoulder. "Right, David, come on, let's get cracking with your room."

Up in Charlotte's room, Eric stands on a chair and unpins a big picture of a dalmatian puppy. "Won't take long to paint these walls. Just give them a wash, then I'll get going – the plaster's sound." He climbs down, rolling up the poster. "Most likely need two coats though," he says.

Jill stands staring at the lime-green walls, then she walks over to the bedside table and picks up the framed photo of Charlotte. "I'll take this into our room," she says.

"No, leave it. I want it!" The words come out louder than I intend and I blush. "Er, if that's all right?" I add more gently.

Jill looks startled but then she smiles. "Of course it's all right," she says. "It's absolutely fine. You're right, Charlie's picture should stay here."

I look at Charlie's photo and think how unfair life is, she had even less time than Mum.

Jill bends and starts gathering up the covers from the bed. "You'll like this room, David," she says in an over-bright voice. "Much more space for you."

I go over and tug at her sleeve. "Are you sure?"

She turns and our eyes meet. "Yes," she says, "I'm sure."

"I'll help with these," Eric says, catching up the corners of the duvet. Together, they fold the bright cover and Eric asks if I want to go with him after lunch to buy paint. When I agree, he strides over to the bookcase and picks up some paint charts. "Here, David. Have a look at these," he says. "Choose your colour."

As I look at the charts, Griffy comes in and jumps up on to the bed. I go and sit beside her and decide on a deep cornflower blue. OK, I know I'm weird, I hated all the blue stuff in my other bedroom but now it's the only colour I want. I look round and imagine everything blue: blue carpet, blue walls.

"Can I move the skateboarding poster in here?" I ask.

Jill laughs and says of course I can and I get quite excited about decorating it with stuff I want. It's a nice room, there's loads more space and lots more light, it'll be good for drawing. Evie Thornton came to see me last week. She brought me a box of pencils and two huge sketch pads. Course she was the one who put the scuds on to me but I don't hold a grudge. Like Jill says, you have to move on.

"Get off that bed, Griffy," Jill says. "Look, she's lying on the bare mattress."

"I don't mind," I say.

"It'll smell of dogs," Jill says.

"No, it won't," I say. "It'll smell of Griffy."

Eric laughs. "You and that dog are of the same breed," he says. "Stubborn as hell."

"I'm not stubborn," I say.

Eric looks thoughtful.

There's a shout from downstairs. It's Sarah. She strides in looking good in a denim skirt and red top. She's taken to wearing colours lately. "Hi," she says. "I've come to help."

"Thanks," Jill replies. "Actually we've nearly finished. David's been fantastic. I couldn't have done it without him."

"It must have been difficult," Sarah says.

Jill shrugs. "It had to be done. I've put it off for too long."

"You weren't ready before," Sarah says.

"No. . . I," Jill says, vaguely. Then she gives a slight shake of her head. "Could you give me a hand with these curtains?"

Sarah climbs up on to a chair and Eric asks me to help him move a bookcase into the middle of the room. When we've done that, I spread an old sheet over it to protect it from paint splashes and Eric goes off to fetch a bucket of water to wash the walls. As I pull down the sheet, I spot a piece of paper lying against the skirting board where the bookcase stood. I go over, pick it up and blow off the dust. Carefully, I unfold it and open it out. It's a kid's drawing, a scribbly picture of a woman with crinkly hair and big glasses, underneath in scrawly writing it says, "My mummy". I glance at Jill but she's oblivious – she's busy pulling out curtain hooks and talking to Sarah. Quickly I re-fold the paper and put it in my pocket.

Sarah bundles a curtain on to the bed, then turns to me. "So are you ready to start school?" she asks.

"I suppose so," I say.

"Great," she says, giving me an encouraging smile. "You're doing fantastic, you know that? It's never easy starting somewhere new. But," she nods, "I know you're going to be OK."

"On Tuesdays we have art," I say.

Sarah reaches for the other curtain. "Good, you'll enjoy that." She gets down and goes to pick up her handbag. "So, are you ready to do my portrait yet?" she asks, pulling out a box of charcoal. "No excuses now," she laughs, waving the box at me.

"OK ," I say.

"We should make a start before Louise gets here or she'll want hers doing too."

Jill laughs. "You'll have to start charging, David."

I scowl, turn my back on them and, calling Griffy, I head for the door. It's news to me that Louise is coming over.

Outside I wander round the back and on to the lawn. Griffy follows me and drops her ball at my feet. I throw it and she does a great acrobatic leap. "Show off!" I tell her.

I throw the ball lots of times then I kick it with Griffy playing goalie. All the while I'm wondering why Louise is visiting. I don't want to talk to her. Don't get me wrong, I like her, she's the best scud I've met but I made my statement, told them what happened. All I want now is for Him to be found guilty, for my evidence to put Him away for a long time.

Griffy drops the ball on my foot and stands there wagging her tail. I pick the soggy thing up and throw it as high as I can, it drops like a stone but she still gets it.

A voice from the window above makes me jump. "Hey, you promised to do my portrait."

I ignore her and throw the ball again.

"That dog is amazing," Sarah says. "Does she ever miss?"

I turn and look up at her. "No," I say.

"I brought some cake," Sarah says. "Why don't you come inside?"

I don't answer, but kick at a stone, sending it scooting across the lawn. I send more stones flying, kick up a hail of gravel, then eventually I get tired of kicking and go in.

Jill and Sarah are sitting at the kitchen table drinking tea.

"Have a piece of cake, it's delicious," Sarah says, pushing a big slice of chocolate cake towards me.

I take the plate and pick off a blob of icing.

"We'll have to save a piece for Louise," Jill says.

The icing coats my tongue.

"You all right, David?" Jill asks.

"Yeah," I say shortly. I pick off some more blobs, they melt in my mouth as I listen for a knock on the door.

The knock doesn't come but I hear Eric clatter downstairs and open the front door. Louise strides in wearing off-duty clothes: tracksuit bottoms and a sweatshirt.

"Hi," she says. "Sorry, to barge in but a couple of things have come up."

"You're always welcome," Jill says. "We're just having tea and cake, would you like some?"

Louise sits down and joins in the tea party.

"So, David, how're you doing?"

"OK."

"Just OK?"

"Fine."

"Good. Are you looking forward to starting school?"

I don't answer.

"He has art on Tuesdays," Sarah says.

"And," Jill says, "he has his pot off next week."

"Wonderful! You'll be back to normal then."

Louise beams at me.

Normal? I sit with my shoulders hunched, flicking at cake crumbs. I'd be more normal if I didn't have scuds visiting me every five minutes.

Louise doesn't seem much like a scud at the moment, though. She's munching cake and talking to Jill and Sarah about the weather and Wimbledon. I wish they'd shut up so she can get down to business. She glances at me and I know she's just biding her time. Sure enough, when she's finished munching, her manner becomes official.

"I just want to go over a few things with you, David. Serious charges are going to be brought against your dad so we have to be sure of our evidence."

I stare at her through narrowed eyes. "What charges?"

She hesitates. "I. . . I can't say at the moment. That's in the hands of the public prosecutor."

"Will he go to prison? Will he get Life?" I ask.

"I don't know, David." She picks up her briefcase. "There are a few points arising from your statement that I want to discuss with you."

I look down at my plate. I don't want to think about him any more. I wish he was in jail for ever, nasty screws kicking him around.

Louise opens a file. "You told us that your dad broke into the house, David. But we haven't found any evidence of a forced entry – a couple of scuff marks on the front door, that's all. How exactly did he break in?"

I stare at the label on the top of the file. MARTIN DAWSON – REFER TO PUBLIC PROSECUTOR.

"How did he get into the house, David?"

I look up; her blue eyes blur and fade.

"David?"

"He broke the door down," I mutter.

"The door wasn't broken, David."

I examine my pot arm. There's lots of drawings on it now.

"David, did your mum let your dad into the house?"

"He killed her," I murmur.

"Did your mum know your dad was coming to visit? Did she invite him in?" Louise asks calmly.

I stare at her. "No," I shout. "I've told you. We didn't know he was coming. He stopped his car, got out, pushed me up the path, then he forced his way in. We couldn't stop him. He wanted to kill her, he said so. He said, if he couldn't have her, nobody could."

Louise's pen is poised over the paper. "I understand. I'm sorry to ask you again, David, but there's one more thing. You told us that your dad dragged your mum on to the landing and then he pushed her down the stairs." She looks at me closely. "Is it possible that your mum fell, David? That she just lost her balance and fell?"

"He meant to do it. I saw him, he shouted he was going to murder her and then he pushed her."

Louise presses her lips together. "And that's the truth?"

"Of course it's the truth. I told you. Why would I tell lies?"

Sarah puts her hand on my arm. "It's all right, David. It's not that they don't believe you. Louise has to ask you these questions, it's her job."

"Your dad claims he never meant to hurt your mum. He says it was an accident, that your mum fell."

Louise watches me all the time, her eyes are floating, zooming in and out. They're the same colour as Mum's eyes. I wish she'd stop staring at me.

David, tell them the truth.

No, Mum, no!

The eyes seem to grow bigger, wider.

David, I want you to tell the truth. Lies are no use. Lies won't bring me back. Only the truth will set you free.

"I wish I'd killed Him," I say.

"Do you?" Louise asks. "Are you sure?"

A strand of hair drops over her forehead, it's almost the same colour as Mum's but not quite so gold. I want to reach out and touch it.

"If I say Mum fell, if I say it was an accident, he'll get off."

"And you don't want that?"

I clench my fist, my breath snorts hot down my nose. "I want him to suffer like Mum did. I want him to pay," I say.

Louise puts out her hand to me, palm upwards. "I think he is suffering, David."

I get up and move away from the table.

"I have to know, David," Louise says. "You are the only witness. Is this statement that you made the absolute truth?"

The room is whirling round me, table and chairs spinning. I feel dizzy. If I close my eyes I'll fall.

Louise's voice cuts through my daze. "David, I understand how hurt you've been, you've been very brave."

She stops as I turn round, open my eyes and glare at

all three of them. I look at them and try to hate them. I think about saying nothing, retreating into silence, just like before. I could stop talking and never speak again. Blood pumps in my ears, I swallow hard.

"No, I haven't," I say. "I haven't been brave at all. If I was brave I'd have stopped Him. I'd have helped Mum. I wouldn't have let her die."

Louise's eyes widen, light glints on the tip of her pen. "Do you think your dad meant to kill your mum?" she asks.

Her voice is clear and sharp as it rings through the still air. She stares at me, fixing me with those blue eyes and I want to run. My foot twitches and my eyes dart to the door. Griffy – alert as ever – picks up my mood, wriggles from under the table and wedges herself against my leg. My fingers tremble as they rake her back. I slide my hand down her front and feel the throbbing of her heart. It's quiet in the room. The women are sitting absolutely still.

I take a long breath in, breathe out, lick my lips and sigh. "No," I say quietly. "No, he didn't mean to kill her." My voice is breaking up but I struggle for control. "Mum tried to stop him hitting me," I say. "She grabbed his arm, he slapped her. She stumbled backwards towards the stairs and then, she fell." I pause and say almost in a whisper, "It was an accident."

In the silence that follows, Griffy lies down, stretches

and sighs. Jill reaches over and puts a hand on my arm. I get up and run shaking from the room.

I fly upstairs, into Charlotte's room and throw myself on the bed. I think I'm going to cry, shed buckets of tears, but I don't. I bang my head on the pillow in frustration. I want the relief of tears but they won't come – perhaps I've used up all my quota, no more left in the tank. I roll over, sit up and look round the room.

The floorboards are bare, all the furniture's shrouded in sheets. Charlotte's photo is the only thing Eric hasn't covered up. I reach into my pocket and take out the drawing. I look at it and want to crumple it up, but I don't. There's a soft knock on the door and Jill comes in.

"I thought I might find you in here."

I don't say anything. She comes over and sits on the edge of the bed. "What's this?" she asks, picking up the drawing. When she looks at it, her face changes. "Oh, Charlie," she says. Tears glisten in her eyes. "Where did you find this?"

"Behind the bookcase when we moved it."

Jill shakes her head. "She was always drawing, loved colour, right from when she was tiny."

"Here," I say, holding out the picture. "You should have it."

Jill's reaches towards it but drops her hand. "No," she says, "This might sound strange but I think you were meant to find it, it's a sort of message. Do you understand?"

I look at her and nod, then I lay the drawing carefully on the mattress. "He won't go to prison now, will he?" I ask.

"I don't know what will happen, David."

"He won't," I say, "They'll let him off."

"He has to live with his conscience," Jill says gently. "That won't let him off."

I stare at her.

"He won't escape," she says. "What he did will haunt him for the rest of his days."

"I hope so," I say.

Jill looks down at the drawing. "David, you have to let go," she says.

"Why?"

"So you can live again." She puts out her hand and strokes my hair. "You've got a lot of living to do."

I pull away. Angry words zoom through my head. I want to yell at her, "If he doesn't go to prison, I don't want to live." But I don't yell. I can't even summon up any real anger. I just feel sad – sad and tired. I close my eyes and Mum's face appears. She's smiling. For the first time in ages I see her really clear, every detail so clear I could draw her.

I open my eyes and smile at Jill. "I want to draw Mum," I say. "I'll draw her and put the picture up over my bed."

"That's a lovely idea," Jill says.

"And I'll put this next to it," I say, pointing to Charlie's drawing.

Jill nods.

"I won't forget my Mum, ever," I say.

"No, of course, you won't," Jill says.

"I can see her now," I say. "I can see her face. When I close my eyes I can remember her, every detail and I'm going to draw her, just how I remember her best."

"How's that?" Jill asks.

"Dancing," I say. "I'm going to draw her dancing."